THE BODY IN THE SHED

A NOVEL

JANET HUBBS

authorHOUSE®

AuthorHouse™
1663 Liberty Drive
Bloomington, IN 47403
www.authorhouse.com
Phone: 833-262-8899

Published by AuthorHouse 04/05/2021

ISBN: 978-1-6655-2164-2 (sc)
ISBN: 978-1-6655-2165-9 (e)

Print information available on the last page.

FOREWORD

So, I'm sitting in a jail cell, in March of the year, an old woman who aches everywhere, sitting in a county jail, a good citizen who has paid her taxes, has never broken the law, has worked hard all her life, raised a model son, loved her two grandsons, me, sitting on a lumpy mattress in a tiny freezing cell. Clank. The cell door shut behind me seconds ago as I got deposited back here to sit after barely eating my breakfast (disgusting oatmeal and watery orange juice, instant coffee) and taking my morning exercise walk of ten minutes around what they laughingly call "the yard"--all too early, too cold, too short. This is a cut-budget, understaffed county jail with many prisoners, some who have probably done terrible things to other people, prisoners with whom I have to breathe the same air and rub up against at various times during the day. We are all women in this wing, but none are my age or even close. Some look like children to me, I can hardly believe they are 18. One of these thin and trembling little-girl types looks as if she will die any minute. When I ask, another prisoner tells me it's withdrawal. From drugs, I guess--but how would I know? This is another planet for me.

One thing we all have in common, though, is that we

are all innocent--or say we are. Except for one lady who readily admits to shooting her husband. But that was self-defense, she says, so she, too, is innocent.

I am supposed to be seeing my lawyer later this morning and all I care about is him getting me out of here. There was some snafu about the bail I was given, something that sent me here rather than home. I don't care. I just want to go home now, because I'm old, I ache everywhere, and I am certainly innocent. But let me start at the start.

PART ONE

1

It's the October before the March I got jailed and I'm home. This particular morning, my coffee tastes like soap. It happens. I get a little too vigorous soaping the glass coffee pot and don't rinse it right or something and then, the next day: soapy coffee. But I'm too lazy to make another pot, so I drink it. It's not poison.

The cats are playing with the plastic container rim from the Halloween candy corn I bought yesterday at the drugstore. They are batting it back and forth between each other, every so often jumping back when it makes the plastic noise that fascinates and scares them. For the cats, everything is a toy, but their lives depend upon the playing, they think. Meanwhile, the gutters continue to fill with leaves, especially this morning because it's windy, autumn windy, leaves swirling everywhere.

The cats stop playing with the plastic to look out the French doors that open from my breakfast room to a small deck; they look at a leaf that hits a door pane, and they contemplate whether or not to attack. But they don't. I am thinking that I should not have bought that candy corn. I bought it to put in a bowl on the kitchen counter as a token decoration, a seasonal touch (I hate Halloween decorations; I hate orange). But I know I will nibble on it, pure sugar, stupid because I don't even like it that much. I do dislike a lot about Halloween, but I love the little teeny weenies in their costumes, often shy and so happy with the candy ("C'n I take two?"). The older kids often have attitude, sometimes embarrassed by doing this for something as nerdy as Kit Kats, Twizzlers, or lollie pops and so don't work too hard on their costumes. One boy last year had on a belted raincoat, flip flops and apparently nothing else. He had a sign around his neck that said "FLASHER." I prefer to believe that 12-year olds don't know what a flasher is, but I'm not stupid. Some have oral-sex and beer parties, I know that, and find it unbearably sad.

The television is on and some people are debating the efficacy of Trump's lies. One commentator says that Trump is a myth-maker, creating stories people love to hear, regardless of facts, truth. I think of what I used to tell my students in a myth course I once taught: Myths are more powerful than truth because people believe them. But it doesn't matter what I think unless I say it on Twitter and thousands of other people re-Tweet me or whatever it is they do. I don't really understand Twitter and its hash tags. But I know it can enable wars, rebellions, spies, and communications between terrorists. Awful things. So cute. A little bird "tweeting." Real birds don't know this and, like knowing about the FLASHER, I wish I didn't know it either. Yet, I continue to read spy novels by Alan Furst and Olen Steinauer and David Ignatius and so I know things, terrible things that I wish I didn't know.

As they say in the *New York Times*: Disclosure. I am

seventy-four years old and tend toward fear. I have always lived in a state approaching anxiety. Not every minute of every day, but through all my life, fear has played its part. Often, I use anger to divert fear, so some people think I have a bad temper. Well, I say, sometimes anger is an appropriate response to certain things. But I also know that anger is more manageable than fear. Someone once said that the best antidote to fear is a plan which may be why I'm also a rather compulsive planner. Why do I need to disclose these things? Because the number of years one has lived and one's world view matter, they both lead to certain thoughts, and fear is a great leveler.

This lends a shade of incredulity to my narrative. People are inclined to think older people live in the past because the present is fleeting and the future uncertain. So the past is more comfortable. But as the young people say, the past is *so over*. The outcome is that older people seem mostly irrelevant. The very idea that older people might know things, that people learn things as they age is passé, a cliché not worth acknowledging, despite the fact that some cultures still honor age That is why I have disclosed my age to you, so that you can consider my narrative irrelevant and decide what to do with it. Candy corn is also rather irrelevant, but people eat it just the same, even if they don't like it.

My story is or was, after all, simple. It's about how to try to do nothing--or, at least, to do what appears to be nothing--and survive. I speak specifically about doing nothing after one retires. I read a lot of books about retirement (written by people who were retired and looking for something to do) and they all say do something, be active, keep moving, get out, volunteer, do crafts, learn a language. Exhausting, really.

One book listed, in alphabetical order, more than three hundred things "to do:" from Acting, Adopt a Highway, Animals, Anthropology, and Antiques to Yodeling, Yoga, Yoyo and Zen. I actually classified this list into three categories: Things I've already done or am doing or am finished with; things I would never do (like Yodeling); and things I might try. In the latter category I found two things I might "do:" De-clutter and Feng Shui. I have done a little of the former (although I don't really have enough clutter to make this matter) and have not yet found a source for the latter, which I barely understand. Am I confusing it with Tai Chi?

I have also read a lot of books by the English writer, Anita Brookner, books in which her characters appear to do nothing--or, at least, not much. I find it fascinating that Ms. Brookner can fill entire novels, critically acclaimed, award-winning novels, theoretically narratives, with central characters who do little and it is a model I am trying to emulate. I know it is anti-American (we Americans are always supposed to be *doing* things) and certainly it is against the advice of the self-appointed retirement specialists. It is also, I might point out, against the advice of physicians and psychologists who repeatedly advocate that an active physical, mental and social life will keep one healthy and youthful. But I reason differently. I reason that as we approach death, we should be able to live, as much as is possible, the life we want to live. I reason it should not necessarily be intensely focused on longevity as much as on what gives us pleasure. This may be selfish, whatever that means, but I think that after working my entire life to measure up to the expectations of others--parents, teachers, family, friends, employers--I should use the time in my diminishing life to do what I want and, maybe even more importantly, not do what I don't want. I'm not grumpy about this.

For better or worse, I am sedentary by nature. It is possible that I inherited this from my father or that I developed it as a side product of other inclinations (like reading and writing). Whatever the case, I do not like exercise and what goes along with it. I am sensitive to extremes of temperature, so as a child, when playing out of doors in winter, especially in the snow, my hands and feet would get cold and numb and eventually painful. No matter how many pairs of socks I put on or how many gloves and mittens I combined on my hands, I would eventually come crying home to my mother with my painful feet and hands, unable to finish building the fort or making the snowman. The other kids did not, as one would expect, tease me about this. They would just get this serious look on their faces and say, softly, the cold makes her feet and hands hurt. My mother would give me hot chocolate and rub my frozen extremities with her warm hands. Conversely, on the stifling New York city sidewalks of July and August, I would suddenly stop sweating and get a kind of clammy and numb feeling and get dizzy, forcing me to run for my darkened house and its breeze from the fans my mother kept running all summer long for just this eventuality. I never gave up, as a child, trying to play outside with my neighborhood friends in either winter or summer, but always eventually surrendered to my bodily protests. It seemed to me that I had no choice.

I was not particularly good at sports, either, and gym class always presented me with a sort of dread. Not only did

I not have the talent for volleyball or soccer or track, I also lacked the stamina. I would just get tired. I was a physically healthy child, not often ill, and except for a terrible time with the measles, missed very little school due to illness. I liked school, did well, and except for gym, was a successful student. I understood the fundamental principles about a *sane mind in a sound body* but just felt I had been short-changed on the sound-body part. I used to take long walks with my father every Sunday and, as long as it wasn't too hot or too cold, enjoyed our walks. My father always had a goal, an objective, for us to see something new or go back to what we'd call "favored places." But what I liked about the walks was talking to my father, not the walking. Solitary walks with no one to talk to did not and still don't interest me.

There was, however, a period of about five years in my life when I did walk every morning, every single morning unless it was pouring rain or the streets were icy. I was in my forties at the time and when I look back now, I can't believe how faithful I was to this daily walking. My alarm would go off and I'd get out of bed and immediately dress for my walk. I bought some athletic clothes and expensive sneakers. I made the coffee and then was out the door within minutes of awakening, my theory being that I was still half asleep, not conscious enough to find excuses for not walking. For several months I would be walking in the dark or semi-dawn, but I had to do it before getting ready for work because I knew I'd never have the energy after I got home from work. I didn't walk long or far, but I walked pretty fast. And then, I just stopped. I'm not sure why.

I decided that given my advancing years, perhaps I had to re-consider exercise. While working, I did not get much--my job a relatively sedentary desk job, but I walked around the office, into other offices, across campus to other buildings--more than I walk around my house since retirement. So I struck out one morning recently, walking for about seven minutes in my immediate neighborhood. By the end of the week I was up to fifteen minutes and, admittedly, feeling more energized upon my return. At the beginning of my second week, I developed a back spasm, the recurrence of a serious back problem I had developed a few years previously. Following the RICE prescription--rest, ice, compression and elevation--I stopped walking in order to observe "rest." I also used ice. The compression and elevation parts didn't seem feasible. My back slowly got better and then I wondered if I had caused it by walking. I haven't walked since and the jury is still out as to whether I'll start again.

Some people get dogs specifically to give them a reason to get out and walk twice a day. I sit at my desk in the morning, looking out my window and down my drive at the road beside my house where the dog walkers go by. The dog walkers like this little lane I live on to walk their dogs because it runs along the river and the views are nice. I love dogs and until seven years ago, always had a dog. But I also have a large, fenced-in yard where my dogs could roam. I only walked them on occasion. For this reason, my dogs were not good walkers, hated the leash, strained against it, and yearned for the freedom of my yard where they could roam and sniff. They were not fond of being walked on a leash along the roadside or being tugged along at will--my will. Of course not.

As for sedentary pursuits, finding watchable TV programs is always a bit of a challenge. I didn't notice this when I was working because I didn't have a lot of free time and always looked for excuses to go to bed early whenever possible. Staying up after 11:00 PM to watch something took a huge effort from me then, knowing the alarm was going to go off at 6:00 AM the next morning. Now--no alarm, no pressure. But sadly, also few good shows at 11:00 PM to tempt me. Even the movies available On Demand are rarely attractive. Occasionally I will gamble on an unknown film and about half the time, regret it. In general, I do not like action films, horror films, or comedies, so that limits the field. I am embarrassed to say that at times I will pay to see a movie I have already seen and liked because I find nothing new appealing. *Syriana* was one of those movies. I saw it in the theater and then twice again On Demand. It's a good movie and a little tricky to follow, and every woman alive loves George Clooney, which I'm sure he knows.

I have decided that while I tend to be a verbal person, I am not a contemplative one. I recall getting dizzy in my philosophy classes in college when subjects like being and nothingness or perception and reality came up. Pondering what was real gave me a headache. I decided then that I lived in a language-based reality, was doomed to do so, and it was real if I could say it. I suppose that's why I liked authors like John Updike so much. Say it; make it real. I think Hamlet ("tell my story") and Nabokov ("if you say it, it will be real"--*Pale Fire*) thought so, too. And it is this about me that makes it hard for me to follow the advice in the retirement books and "do something." Doing things that are non-verbal do not seem like "something" to me. They do not seem real. And two other things: They require that I be at a certain place at a certain time regularly; and most are incredibly boring (like handing out newspapers to people in hospital beds who could care less about the news).

And so I had settled, or so I thought, into a rather sedentary life after my retirement, a life in which I didn't think too much about "doing something," a life punctuated by simple activities and small pleasures and my nice house and my two cats, some good friends, some shopping, a little travel, a quiet and rather satisfying existence. At times, I wished for a little more, a little excitement perhaps? Be careful of what you wish for.

2

Halloween is over now and so are Thanksgiving and Christmas, as attenuated as they were, and you will be surprised, as I was surprised, to learn that something startling and horrific actually happened in my life after Halloween but before both the big holidays, something more than watching my cats play with plastic wrappers or having lunches or dinners with my friends. I found a body. I found a dead body in my potting shed.

I didn't find the complete body, I must be quick to say. I actually smelled it and then glimpsed it and then called the police who did the full physical discovery.

It was like this: The first week in November I was finally taking the last of some summer detritus out to the potting shed in the far back corner of my property--flower pots, a wind chime that rattles annoyingly in the autumn breezes, a few cheerful plaques that say "Welcome" and "Summertime" which I hang on the house walls around my decks. As I approached the potting shed which I had not been near for weeks, I smelled something foul and rotten and I watch enough of ID (the murder channel) on television to know that there might have been cause for alarm. I slowed down, set my junk on the path and went slowly to the door of the shed. I opened it a bit, aware that the smell was now truly awful, and peeked around the door which is when I saw the leg--a man's leg in khaki trousers with a black boot on the foot--and that was all I saw. That was enough. I turned and I think I must have raced back to the house and just immediately dialed 911. I have no clear recollection of doing this. But I do recall that the 911 lady was a bit dense and I kept having to repeat to her what I smelled and saw and she kept asking unanswerable questions and asking me if I were *sure.* She asked me if anyone was in my house and told me to stay on the phone until the police arrived--and it was about then that I started shaking and could hardly talk or hold the telephone any more.

The police seemed to come very fast or perhaps time had telescoped for me, but the next thing I knew they were there--three police cars--probably the whole on-duty force for our small town. Two policemen were at my front door and two were at the side door and I didn't know which door to answer, I remember thinking, but finally went to the side door as it was closest and suddenly my breakfast room was full of these two huge uniformed young men. They seemed confused about why they were there so I told them again directly about the smell and the body, let them out through the French doors on to the deck, pointed down the path toward the shed, and just stood there until I remembered the policemen at the front door--and then went to let them in as well. Same thing--told them--took them out and pointed them in the direction of the shed. I think the remaining two officers from the third patrol car were roaming about my property, but I could be wrong about that as events in my memory start to blur at this point.

My next conscious clear memory is of me sitting at my breakfast room table with one of the policemen giving him information, first about me--and then about my discovery. He asked me who the man was, did I know him, but I told them I had only gotten as far as seeing his foot and leg, had no clue. At some point, two plain clothes policemen arrived who were detectives or maybe some sort of county or state police, I'm not sure, asked me the same questions the policeman had asked me and then, eventually, a medical van of some sort came to pick up the body. One of the detectives asked me to view the remains to see if I knew the victim and I just felt as if I might vomit--but I agreed to do it. They had him in the van by this time and just unzipped the face part of the black plastic bag and, no, I did not know him at all, I told them. He was filthy and, of course, dead, so I guess I said I didn't recognize him. The detective pressed me when I said that and then I vomited in the van--and so they took me back into the house and let me clean up and told me to have a drink. I think I was shaking again. I had Scotch, which I don't drink anymore, but it was the first bottle in the liquor cabinet that came to hand and so I poured a little and drank it. I thought I might vomit again, but I didn't.

The detectives stayed and asked many more questions and then said would I come down to the police station and talk more. I asked if I could come in the morning and they said yes, yes. They also told me a crime scene crew was in the potting shed and would probably be there for a few more hours--and that they might remove a few things. Just to let me know. And then they asked if I would please stay out of the shed until advised otherwise--as if I would go near the place. And then, finally, they left. I noticed a police car remained outside my house which was the first time that I thought I myself could be in danger.

Someone had put a body in my potting shed. Who was the body and who had put him there--and why in my shed? I was very dizzy and nauseous and I knew I should be afraid, but somehow I couldn't feel fear--my primary emotion--or even anger. And then I remember looking at the clock and seeing it was almost 8:00 PM. I think I had found the body a little after 2:00 PM. So I had had six hours of this craziness and the time had passed so quickly that I was stunned when I saw that it was 8:00 o'clock. I finally made some tea, ate some toast, and just sat in my breakfast room, remembering, ordering the memories, wondering if I should call someone, talk to someone. I even had a vague notion that perhaps I should call my lawyer to go with me to the police in the morning. I finally called Martha, my closest friend, and tried to tell her about it--but she already knew. It had been on the local radio news and she had been just about to call me. They didn't mention my name or specific address on the news broadcast, but gave the general location and mentioned the potting shed and Martha was positive that it was me. She was gratifyingly horrified for me, did not make me recount the grisly details, and offered to go with me to the police station in the morning. That sounded very good to me so we arranged that she'd pick me up and we'd go together. She also asked about a lawyer but I said it didn't seem to fit the circumstances.

After we hung up, I suddenly remembered my cats and went looking for them. Oh God, please that they didn't get out in all the fuss. They are indoor cats and never ever go out. I wandered down the back hall screeching their names and both appeared peeking out of my bedroom door, my bedroom where they had been, I was sure, under the bed, their favorite hiding place, all this time. They ran down the hall to me--meowing loudly as they ran, and I scooped both up at once, very unusual for me and not good for my back, but I suddenly wanted to bury my face in them and feel how warm they were. Oh kitties, I said, Mommy has had a really bad day.

After a while they squirmed and I let them down and they ran into the kitchen, suddenly starving and meowing to be fed. Two cute little tabby cats, alive, not dead in the shed.

I finally went to bed about 10:00 PM. I did not watch ID, one of my favorite TV channels all about, ironically, murder, and I did not sleep well. No wonder. I was up before 6:00 AM and took a very hot shower and washed my hair for longer than usual, shampooing and rinsing three times--for no reason except that I irrationally believed that I still had a tinge of the dead smell about me and had to wash it away. I took care with styling my hair, doing my make-up, dressing in what I hoped would be appropriate clothing for a police inquiry (indeed something new under my sun) and then made a pot of coffee, fed the cats, and sat drinking many cups of coffee pondering, sorting my feelings. I was not surprised to feel fear, my default feeling, after all. The police car was still there--or perhaps another one was there having traded out with the guy who started the surveillance--and this still spelled danger to me. Perhaps it was not an arbitrary act dumping that body in my shed. Perhaps it was somehow aimed at me, the first act in what might become a series of terror tactics. Why? I barely had friends let alone enemies and any despicable act I had ever committed was so far in my past as to make vengeance an extremely suspect motive. I live such a quiet life that I barely make a ripple, so who could have it in for me? And then anger took over. Just as I had settled on "nothing" as my inevitable and thus preferred lifestyle, someone thought to dump a dead body in the middle of it. Just as I was taking stock and thinking nothing much could or would ever change for me, it had.

It was in this state of mind that Martha found me when she came to get me and take me to the cops--looking all bright and efficient as Martha always does. She is a tall person of considerable presence. She wears her long brown hair pulled back severely into a stylish knot and always has on some kind of dangly earrings. She is slim and what people call "athletic" looking--good posture, healthy shape. She has few wrinkles and looks to me as she did at 50 or even 40, we have been friends that long. She was wearing her jeans and a sweater coat thing that looked chic. Martha always looked that way. What the hell's with the cop car, she asked, and I told her I guessed it was either for my protection or to be sure I stayed put--or both. Who knows, I said. This is just so incredible and I am getting more and more pissed, you know? She again asked me if I was sure I didn't need a lawyer and I said that we'd see how the interrogation went and that if I felt threatened, at all, I'd just shut up and get a lawyer to come.

We made the short drive down to the police station in the middle of town. It was a small town and the police department was housed in the town hall in the town center, a red brick building with white trim, surrounded by big oaks and some pine trees. Martha and I went into the side entrance that had a big globe light with the letters MTPD over the door and presented ourselves at the desk or counter, sort of both in one. I identified myself and was quickly ushered by a large lady cop into a room down a short hall with a table and four chairs, two on either side of it (and nothing else) and a big clock on the wall where I was to await my 9:00 AM appointment. Martha waited outside on a little wooden bench in the hallway.

At 9:10, one of the plainclothes policeman with whom I had talked the day before came in, shuffling some papers, looking very spiffy, with the kind of spit and polish policemen and military men always seem to have. He was sort of young, I'd guess about 40-45, although I'm not good at guessing ages anymore. He was medium height, a bit heavy or square or muscular, whatever you call it, and had dark short hair and a pleasant face, regular features, very flat ears. He wore khaki pants and a blue blazer with a pale blue shirt and striped tie. He was a very comfortable looking man and I guess this was part of the deal--put me at ease, for whatever merciful or nefarious reasons. He read through his papers for a minute after giving me a brief smile, then patted them all together, set them down on the table, extracted one from the pile, and began to talk. He informed me that our session was being recorded and since I seemed to have no choice in the matter, I didn't say anything. Next, he reviewed my personal details that I had given to the uniform the day before, confirming the information that was essentially minimal and correct. Yes, full name, yes, birth date, yes address and telephone, yes, yes, and yes.

He then produced a photograph of the face of the body

(as I had taken to calling him)--essentially the same as the live (or dead) view I had seen the day before in the van, right before I vomited, but the face in the picture was cleaner, as though someone had tidied him up a bit. I looked, and then looked up at Detective Eggers (as he told me to call him) and he asked, rather gently I thought, if I was still unable to identify the man. I looked at the picture again and concentrated--I really did want to be helpful--and then just said, no, I have never seen this man before. I was thinking of a million disclaimers--such as--I had been a college teacher for more than thirty years, had had hundreds of students during those years and was certain I would not remember half of them, by face, if I were to see them again today, especially after so much time had elapsed. But I didn't say this. I just let my unqualified "no, never" answer hang in the air. I seemed to remember hearing on maybe ID or *Law and Order* that you should just keep your answers short and truthful.

And while I looked down at that picture of that dead face, I am not sure I even ever saw "him" as a person, let alone a person I knew. The face seemed to me as if it were bloated, the mouth gaped a little and the head seem shaved or naturally bald, I couldn't tell. It seemed oddly ageless in one way, neither old nor young, but in another way seemed very, very old. I had this fleeting thought that I could not actually believe this face had ever been a living thing, always and forever "the body" to me.

Detective Eggers then went on to what seemed like a slight digression, asking me if I could think of anyone who would want to do me harm or would target me by doing something like this. No, I said, no one at all. I said that rather quickly so he asked me to think about it and I did--and still said, after the interval of thought: No, really. This is just such a terrible thing, I don't think I know anyone who would do anything to either the poor dead man or to me. No one. I did offer an additional thought by saying I truly believed that my potting shed was just a location of opportunity and had nothing to do with me personally. Just a body dump, I thought to myself.

Detective Eggers then told me that they were estimating the time of death some three days prior to my discovery and asked if I could remember any particular disturbances on that day, did I have anyone at the house--and, by the way, where had I been and what had I been doing. That would have been Sunday, I asked? Yes, Sunday. So I gave a full account of my day--some of which could be verified, some of which could not, all truthful--church, lunch with a friend (name of friend given), football on TV, dinner at home, book and bath in the evening and a little Sunday Night football, until I fell asleep--and said I could not recall even the slightest disturbance or deviation from the norm on that day or evening or night. Of course, I am usually asleep by ten o'clock, so could not attest to anything after that time. I tend to be a sound sleeper.

I noticed that Detective Eggers did not tell me the cause of death or the identity of the body, but I assumed that they were still not sure of the former--the medical examiner's report and all that--and probably did not yet know the latter, lest why the picture identification drill? Naturally I was curious, but was also certain that this information would be available in the newspapers and on the radio as soon as it was disclosed--and doubted they'd disclose to me much before they told the press. Detective Eggers then moved on to ask me about people with access to my property and who accessed it regularly. I mentioned my gardener, my lawn sprinkler people, the pond maintenance man, and my cleaning lady--and also pointed out that since the gates were never locked, technically, the world had "access" if they chose to wander on in. He also asked me, as if he had forgotten, if my shed could be viewed from the lane that ran along the side of my property or from the front. The shed is visible from the side lane, but not from the front road, I told him. He asked me the approximate size of my property and I told him it was about a half an acre but that the woodland at the rear of the property was not developed. He asked what was behind that woodland. Well, the fence extends around the lawn to the edge of the woods, I answered, and behind the fence is the woods and the land that slopes down to the river. But, I mean, there aren't any houses or other outbuildings there, I added. He asked me if I had river access. I didn't understand the question. Can you access the river by walking through the woods. Oh, yes, I said, there's a little path that goes down. There's a gate in the back fence where that path starts. I was going to add that I had the fence put in for my dog, now deceased, who had been a runner. But I didn't say that. No point. I was also going to tell him that I had a river view when the leaves were off the trees in the fall and winter--a partial view right now as the leaves were falling, but I guessed he knew that. Certainly the policemen who roamed my property for hours the day before would have sketched all that out?

He seemed about to leave and then paused to ask me a little about my "background," as he put it. Where was I born, educated, what about family, marriage, children. I gave a brief synopsis, straight forward and boring--born in New York City, educated in city public schools and Columbia University, no siblings, parents of course deceased, extended family in England where my parents were born, two marriages, both husbands deceased, a son living in San Diego with his wife and two children. He seemed momentarily interested in my son, as if that made me more a part of the human race than previously expected, and I told him that my boy was the child of my first marriage, had been a naval officer, and was now retired and working as an investment advisor in California at age fifty. He didn't push for details beyond that, only asking when I had last seen my son. I told him of the annual summer visit in July--my son and his family always come home to the Jersey shore every summer and stay with me for two weeks--and that I was due to fly to San Diego for Christmas. OK, lady. Enough of you. He didn't say that--just smiled and thanked me for my time. He said something about being in touch--did they have my contact information? of course they did!--and if I had to be out of town, to please let them know. And, oh, the police tape would be down soon.

As I walked out of the interview room, I realized I was perspiring rather heavily. I hadn't noticed it while we were talking and it hadn't occurred to me that the room was especially hot, but now as I walked out of the little room back to where Martha was still sitting on the bench, I could feel little rivulets of perspiration rolling through my hair. I always sweat from my head--no antiperspirant yet developed for the scalp! I was hoping that Detective Eggers hadn't noticed the persrpitatopm as I said to Martha, OK, all done, let's get out of here.

Martha and I decided to go out for brunch for a de-brief, as Martha called it. Over an omelet for her and pancakes and sausage for me (comfort food), I told her all I could remember about the interview. I sat looking around the pretty little garden restaurant we'd chosen for our meal and felt that the previous hour now had an aura of deep unreality. *This* was my life: friends, food, pretty little restaurants--not a police station and a Detective Eggers. I tried to shake it off and took comfort from Martha telling me that none of the interview sounded terribly threatening. I mean, she said, I suppose that they had to check on your whereabouts or alibi or whatever they call it--but how in hell could you ever kill someone and get him into the shed. Or, I asked, what if I killed him in the shed? I was playing Devil's advocate, but Martha took me seriously and said--oh, yeah, um--and stopped eating. You know, I said, I didn't even ask if it was a murder. I mean, what if he was just a bum hanging out in my shed for shelter and had a heart attack or something? How stupid! I suddenly felt vulnerable in the fact that I had so easily and obviously suspected murder all along, even though I hadn't asked or said this to the detective. How bad had that looked? Judging from the slight frown on Martha's pretty face, I realized I had opened up a whole new chasm for bad thoughts.

Oh let's just eat and forget it, Martha said. Too many ifs. You told the truth. You had every reason to suspect foul play what with the cops and crime scene tape all over the place. I mean, I know you can't really forget it--but just let it go. You already had your interrogation. Don't start interrogating yourself. And Martha was right. We ate, drank more coffee, paid up and then Martha dropped me home before noon. The tape was still up, but the patrol car was gone. So I just thanked Martha, promised to keep her posted, went on in, dropped my stuff carelessly on a little chest just inside the side door and exhaled.

I knew--had known all last night and this morning--that I should call my son. I mean, we were not phone chatterers and usually only talked at length about once a month or briefly if we had business to discuss, but surely this extraordinary event merited a phone call? I always believed that my problems were my problems and that I could manage them without involving my son, without bothering him unless he were indeed involved. I never discussed small health matters, only mentioned the significant ones--but, really, how much could he ever do for me, three thousand miles away? Nonetheless, on the off chance that somehow the news of the body should reach him from another source, he would definitely be angry, hold me to account, if I failed to call.

As I pondered this, the phone rang and remarkably it was my son who did in fact know the story, learned it from reading an online report in a local paper, from an app that he kept on his phone and checked from time to time, to stay abreast of news from the land of his childhood. And he was angry, very angry. So Jared, I said, I was just about to call you. I had to see the police this morning and I wanted to wait until the interview was over before I called so that I could fill you in. I invented as I went along but it seemed plausible to him apparently, as he shut up. Then he asked me what my lawyer had said and then started another round of invective as I told him I had not involved Terrance, my lawyer. God, mother! But look, Jared, I'm not even sure there's a crime here. I mean, what if the guy was just a vagrant who happened into the shed for shelter and had a heart attack or something? They never said anything about cause of death or homicide or suspicious death or whatever and I just don't know what to think or do. What you are going to do is to call Terrance as soon as we hang up and what you are going to think is what Terrance tells you to think. Understood? I hate when he talks to me this way, but I grudgingly agreed that he was right, that all the *Law and Orders* ever shown on the tube don't give real-world advice on these matters. So I agreed. Terrance was a high school friend of Jared's who had stayed in the local area, a nice and pleasant man who practiced family law, but was in a practice with partners who handled criminal cases--so he could either advise me himself or put me together with a partner who could. After settling the lawyer business, Jared and I chatted a bit for a while longer, smoothing down edges, giving love, and parted friends.

I looked up Terrance's office number, called, and was not surprised to find him unavailable. The secretary offered me a 3:00 PM call-back and I said fine. I'd be home; call the land line. I was not hungry for lunch as I had just devoured those pancakes a few hours ago, so I made a cup of tea and took it out on the deck to drink. It was an unseasonably warm day for early November, a kind of autumn-hazy day with lukewarm sun and no breeze, over sixty degrees. I sat and looked north to the property next door. It had been purchased by a young couple who had knocked down the small cottage that had inhabited that property for more than fifty years, a summer home mostly, a couple who were now embarked on building their dream home. I had met them very briefly a few times and they were a very nice couple and quite conscientious about sending me texts and keeping me up to date with the building process, being "good neighbors" they said. It was an ultra modern home--very geometric and filled with glass walls and stark-looking decks angled to catch river views. According to Mariah, the wife, the project would be more than a year in the making.

They had started in the spring and by now, although the outlines of what would be the home were very distinct, it was still more or less a shell, with huge piles of dirt surrounding it. I watched with moderate curiosity. It was not a home I would be comfortable living in, huge and certainly an oddity in our very conventional little town where most home styles were more traditional, but I have always had great interest in those stark modern styles, find them artistic and dramatic, places I would like to visit and be entertained in. This one was poured concrete and metal and glass, from what I could tell and was two stories on one side and three on the other, as it was built on the side of a hill. I watched lazily as workmen went back and forth. I had been dreading the start of construction as I was sure it would be noisy and intrusive, but it was a reasonable distance away from my house, and I had been pleasantly surprised at how little I had been aware of the construction. At times, I'd hear an unfamiliar noise on our otherwise very quiet road and would become aware that it was part of the building process, but this was rare and almost always non-intrusive. It was the same today. Lots of activity as I watched, but only muted sounds arising out of the autumn haze.

I then had a thought and wondered if by any chance the body could be related to the construction. Maybe a worker, down on his luck, had spotted my shed and sought shelter there and then died? Could that be? The building seemed to require several specialized crews, many consisting of men who did not speak English from what I could overhear from a distance, and so if the body were a member of one of the crews, perhaps a lonely immigrant, a crew that had already finished its work, no one would necessarily note his absence, would they? Maybe I should have told detective Eggers or should call him? I was almost up and off the chaise before I remembered Jared's advice to let Terrance do the thinking and so I thought, well, I'll just mention this to Terrance, and went back to sitting, drinking my tea, and watching the little figures in the distance go about the business of building a house.

I must have dozed off because suddenly I was startled by a noise, a kind of whooshing sound that woke me and then frightened me until I looked up and saw two uniformed policemen half-stooped over one of the flower beds near my deck. I got up and walked over to the railing of the deck and one of the men looked up and seemed to jump a little--as perhaps I had startled him as much as he had startled me. I didn't recognize either of them from yesterday and then noticed that they were not locals but maybe state troopers. I asked if I could do anything for them but they just smiled congenially--the startled one laughing a little and saying no thank you ma'am, that they wouldn't be much longer. I hate being called ma'am, but they did identify themselves and were very polite, so I returned their civility. I returned to my chaise but by then I was too uncomfortable to resume my nap or my gazing, so went back into my house. It turned out to be almost 3:00 PM anyway--and so I assumed Terrance would be calling soon.

He did, on the stroke of three, and we talked for almost half an hour. The upshot was that he took all the information, thought my interview that morning had probably just been routine, not to worry, but told me if the police wanted another interview, I should refer them to him and he'd handle it. I was not obliged to talk to them any further or, in fact, at all. I mean, I said, I want to help them, but I don't know what else I can do. Exactly, Terrance said, which is why you shouldn't do anything, except be sure your premises are secure, doors locked, alarms on, and call 911 at the slightest disturbance. And remember, he said again, as though I was apt to forget, no more chats with the cops, safe, sorry. Yes. Got it. We arranged for me to send in a check as a retainer--I insisted on paying the going fee, no favors for family of friends, I laughed--and Terrance said he'd contact me if he needed anything else. And no more talking to police, he said, as his closing comment, now a refrain. I could see that I probably should never have talked at all--stupid--but my conversation with Terrance made me feel more stabilized, more normal than I had in the past day and, I don't know, more protected or something.

I thought about going out to see if the police or troopers or whoever they were had gone or were still nosing around, but I thought better of it. I didn't want to be--or to look like--the proverbial nosey old lady and also had already started internalizing the "avoid the cops" mentality that both my son and Terrance thought to be so important. I was just curious to see if that annoying yellow tape had been taken down. No one had told me to honor it or not to cross it or anything, but it still made me feel uncomfortable, like a trespasser in my own home.

I decided, after declining to go out and check on the policemen, to play what I called my Scarlet O'Hara game. This consisted of refusing to think about something nasty or worrisome by saying, in Scarlet fashion, "I'll think about it tomorrow." Over the years, I had gotten pretty good at this denial technique or whatever it was and found I was often able to put away troubling thoughts by just repeating Scarlet's mantra enough times until I indeed found myself thinking of something else. In this case, it was dinner. I hadn't thought to take anything from the freezer but I also hadn't had lunch due to the big brunch with Martha. I was getting hungry. So I decided to drive down to the fish market and get a piece of fresh fish for my dinner. I don't love fish, but understand that it is good for me and also find that once I prepare it, it actually tastes better than I thought it would taste. I was thinking maybe flounder, to fry, breaded and crispy, or salmon, to bake with lemon butter and parsley. Or maybe I'd get creative and make sole Veronique as I still had some green grapes in a bowl on the kitchen counter. As I drove over the bridge and parked at the fish place, I was still thinking of fish and recipes and that is perhaps why I didn't notice a familiar car--a big red Cadillac, who could miss it!-- parked outside the shop. If I had noticed it, I might not have gone in, for the car belonged to a woman I knew, could not really call a friend, who was quaintly known as the town gossip. She was not really malicious, just a huge blabbermouth and hard to get away from until she was satisfied she had wrung every detail out of a person on her subject *de jour*. Shit, I thought, as soon as I saw her, Mona, at the counter. And of course she spotted me and of course she wanted to know *all about* the body and oh my dear how gruesome for you. I quickly ordered two pieces of flounder from the clerk, all thoughts of delicate fish cuisine flown and tried for the ensuing five minutes while my order was filled to tell Mona nothing. I kept saying there wasn't much to tell and then she'd ask something else--did you actually see the cadaver? did you have to go to the police station? did you know who the dead guy was? how did he die? I finally got and paid for my fish and just smiled at Mona saying that she had more questions than the police, ha-ha-ha. She replied by saying that she was surprised that I hadn't been *deluged* by reporters, camped out on your lawn, I would've thought. Oh my dear. Bye-bye privacy. I sort of backed out of the store, saying uh-huh, uh-huh, trying to smile and wave her away and when I finally got to my car and made the short drive home, there on my front lawn, making Mona prophet as well as gossip, were a gaggle of reporters and even one guy with a hand-held TV camera. Glory days.

I just opened my garage door remotely, drove in, shut the door from inside my car and waited for the door to go down before I exited into my garage and from there into my house. After putting the flounder into the fridge, I walked around slowly and methodically, drawing closed all the blinds on windows exposed to "the press." I was aware of some shouting, questions, but just sort of blotted everything out and turned on the TV to further drown out the noise. Of course the TV was on a local news station and of course, I picked the exact moment they were doing the story on the body, and of course on my TV screen at that precise moment was ta-da! a video of my house, the yellow tape, and the parts of my property that could be seen from the road and the lane. The video made my house look lovely, larger than life, but somehow strange. It didn't look like my house to me. Quickly, I just changed the channel to cable news which at least, at that point, had no interest in the body or my property and were doing some follow-up story on Trump.

3

The next morning, Friday, the reporters were gone, at least for the time being, the tape had come down, and as I walked around my house, opening blinds and some French doors for a moment to let in some fresh air, cooler now, I had the feeling that life could and would, and perhaps already had, returned to normal. I fed the cats and then made my bed as I waited for my coffee to brew. I thought about my day, noted on my calendar that the HVAC guys were coming in the afternoon to do the semi-annual inspection--fall for heat, spring for air conditioning--and decided I would spend the morning doing some mindless housework and then perhaps, perhaps, go out back and see what things looked like at the crime scene or body dump zone or whatever it might be called--my potting shed. But, only perhaps. I had this irrational fear that the smell of human decay would still be lingering in the autumn air and had no particular desire to encounter it.

I put on jeans and a tee shirt and did my room-to-room light housekeeping. This consisted of going into each room of my house with a dust rag and Pledge and the handi-vac, swiping bureaus or table tops, straightening anything out of order, vacuuming floors and carpets, and making a mental note of anything that needed further attention--replacements, additions, future projects. I would make note of these things and they served as a new "to do" list for my consideration. My house was always clean because my housekeeper came once a week and saw to the heavy cleaning; and it was usually neat because many of the rooms were essentially unlived in. My bedroom and bath, the kitchen, my office and the breakfast room were where I mostly hung out--and from time to time, the living room and the sun room where I would read or watch television. The two guest rooms and the dining room were never used unless I had guests and, because I am a neat person, the rooms I did use were straightened after use. Nonetheless, I liked my "room to room" inspections as on site guarantees that my domain was in order.

I had just finished this project which took less than an hour when the front doorbell rang. I wasn't expecting anyone until the HVAC people in the afternoon, and suddenly my brain said: cops, reporters, oh no! And I almost didn't answer the door, but then I did and was surprised to find Mariah, my soon-to-be new next door neighbor, on my front steps. She was a striking woman in many ways, perhaps late thirties? She was thin almost to the point of emaciation with cheek bones that jutted out of an otherwise unremarkable face except for enormous green eyes heavily surrounded by make up, the smoky eye look on steroids. She had shoulder length reddish-brown hair, thick and totally and absolutely straight, with a slash of bangs across her forehead that brought even more attention to those eyes. She was of average height, but looked taller, I suppose because of how thin she was. She was dressed this morning in black jeans and black boots and a huge fisherman sweater and looked, as I suppose she intended, like a runway model for big sweaters.

Oh my goodness, Mariah, I said over her apologies for intruding without calling, come in, come in, so nice to see you. I had this fleeting thought out of nowhere that I could be inviting a murderer in--a thought that perhaps I'd have for some long time to come about everyone who crossed my threshold--but blotted it out and brought Mariah into the breakfast room and sat her down with a cup of coffee. I asked how the house was going and told her how nice it looked but then stopped my chatter when it became obvious to me that she wanted to talk about something and that this was not just a social call. And of course what she wanted to talk about was the body. She confessed that she and Tad, her husband, had been badly shaken by the reports--and kindly acknowledged that she could not even imagine how horrible it had been for me--and then went on to say or to ask if it was possible for me to tell them anything that might in some way or another be reassuring.

I really didn't find this all that intrusive--even as she kept apologizing for being intrusive--because I could understand both her concern and her curiosity. It was, after all, her neighborhood--or neighborhood to be. On the other hand, I was mentally cautious recalling everything that Terrance had stressed and so told Mariah very little that she could not have read in the papers--but did so in a friendly and cooperative way--like, oh, yes, of course you are concerned--but I really know so little. I told her how I observed the leg of the body, left out the bit about the smell, called the police, and spoke to them on two occasions at which time they disclosed nothing. I don't even know the cause of death, I was careful to say, not wanting to make any assumptions that might be suggestive of anything at all. No, I didn't recognize the dead person and had been told zero about him by anyone. Mariah said the reporting on TV and the morning papers suggested that he might have been a vagrant but that the police were calling the cause of death "suspicious," so there was still much to be discovered. Well, I said, I avoided looking at the TV coverage last night and hadn't yet seen today's papers, so that she seemed to know more than I--or, at least the press did. She seemed a little surprised at my ignorance and gently pressed me with a few more questions--how was he dressed, how old did he seem. I told her what I had seen--one leg, khaki pants and a black boot--and that I had no idea how old he might be--just bald, or at least hairless, and very dead, thus hard to tell.

She continued with her feelings--of sympathy for my "ordeal," as she kept calling it, and of concern for her and Tad and their "investment." I raised my hands, palms up, and said we'd probably find out everything eventually--you know, all the criminal science tools today are remarkable, little microscopic bits and pieces of evidence opening doors to vast universes of evil. She raised an eyebrow at that comment, so I laid off the poetics and said that I seriously did not think the property values would be affected for any length of time. This will end and people will forget--and you will have your lovely house on a pretty road in a nice town. Well, what could I say? I had already thought a bit about my own house taking on the "murder house" label, but since I had no plans to sell or move, what did I care?

Mariah stayed for another little while. She offered some details on minor problems with their building project, but I resisted asking her if any of her workers were missing. Terrance would have been proud. She said she and Tad were thus far satisfied with the builders on the whole--and that the project seemed to be on schedule. They were still hoping to move in during April or May of the following year. And then we finished our coffee, exchanged a hug, and she was on her way.

After she left, I thought, well, that was actually kind of odd. I had only met Mariah twice in the past, once when she stopped by to introduce herself and tell me about their plans to take down the cottage and build a new house, and once when I was out gardening and she was driving by--stopping when she saw me to give a brief progress report on their house project and then be on her way. She was nice and friendly, although not the warm or chatty type, but that was fine with me. It was Tad, her husband, who texted me from time to time, but nothing along those lines from Mariah. Good fences make good neighbors. So was her visit today a little weird? Out of character? I just shrugged it off. Probably not too weird. Curiosity gets us all.

Just then the telephone rang and I hesitated to answer it. Would it be the cops? Reporters? TV news people? Would I be afraid to answer my phone for the duration until the body thing was over? I let it go to message anyway, caution reigns, and it turned out to be Jared, my son, so I picked up and said hi, monitoring my calls. Suddenly there are all sorts of calls I don't want to get. He agreed this was wise and then of course asked me if I had talked to Terrance and made arrangements. I told him I had and he was pleased, sounding as though he never quite expected me to take his very good advice or follow his very explicit directions. He was on his way to work, calling from the car, just wanting to check in before he started his day. Apparently happy with all of what I told him, including the phone monitoring, he gave me love--love you, Mom--said cheery bye, and was off to work, making money for people. Or so he hoped.

I had just turned away from the phone when it rang again and in a sort of reflex action, thinking it was Jared calling back, I picked it up and answered it. As soon as I said hello, I thought, damn. But it was too late. And really too bad as well, as it was Detective Eggers, of all people. Double damn. I hadn't really rehearsed whatever little speech I would make in case he called, so I kind of stammered into the phone, as soon as he identified himself, how very sorry I was and how very much I wanted to help, but on advice of counsel, I was supposed to refer all calls concerning this matter to him, to counsel--and then I found myself rifling through my drawer to find the damn address book and then scrambling through my address book looking for Terrance's contact information. My heart seemed to be beating too fast and for some reason I seemed to have forgotten Terrance's last name, so I stopped, took a deep breath, and then found what I was looking for: Terrance Hannity, Esq. with all the pertinent information. Detective Eggers seemed neither particularly surprised nor annoyed, just waited quietly there on the other end of the phone and then took the information I supplied, thanked me and hung up. I suppose they're probably used to people "lawyering up" these days, I thought, with lawyers all over television telling people to do that. I didn't particularly like having done it on the "if you have nothing to hide" argument. But, well, my son and then Terrance had been so firm on this point, no choice. I suppose I was a sort of a "person of interest" to the police--my potting shed after all. But, honestly, the idea of the police suspecting me, even marginally, me, a harmless little old lady, seemed vaguely absurd. And, I kept having to tell myself, I did not yet even know whether or not a crime had been committed. Perhaps Detective Eggers had called to tell me the man had died of natural causes or that they knew who he was--or both--case closed. Oh well, if that really were the case, which I doubted, magical thinking, Terrance could tell me just as well.

Later that day, as I recall, the HVAC guys came and did their inspection, tightened this, cleaned that, replaced filters, and told me all was well and that I could approach the coming winter confident that I'd be warm and toasty. I love those kinds of things, where no one tells you that you have this awful problem that will take tons of time and money to fix. I have had those, too, so always appreciate the efficient, no-problem service visits. They leave me elated. Warm and toasty is better than freezing to death because your heating system went south while you were fast asleep.

The weekend was uneventful, as I recall, and I guess I passed it peacefully. Until Monday morning, when Terrance Hannity called and I got a near-terminal case of the jitters.

He said he had spoken with Detective Eggers and it seems as though two things were true: The man in the shed had in fact been murdered, shot; and it appeared that I might have known him after all. So, Terrance wanted to talk to me about this and get some facts straight and, no, I didn't have to talk with the police again at this time (I didn't like the implications of the "at this time" disclaimer), but as my lawyer, he needed more information. First, did I or had I ever owned a firearm of any sort? No, I said, never. The one and only gun I had ever seen up close or touched was my first husband's service revolver when he was in the Navy. We had lived in Florida at the time, off the Naval Air Station in a house in the woods, and there was a rapist-killer at large which had the whole city of Pensacola in a panic. My husband had grudgingly left me the gun for "protection," but took out the clip so, as he said, "you don't shoot the mailman." I was supposed to point it at the assailant in the unlikely case that he should appear in order to scare him off. He presumably would not know it had no bullets. But that was fifty years ago, I said. And after my husband got out of the Navy, we never had a firearm again. And, my husband has been dead for more than 30 years.

OK. Terrance next asked: Does the name Mortimer Arthur mean anything to you? I thought about that because the name sounded familiar. Mortimer Arthur, Morty Arthur. Oh my goodness, I said, yes. I went to grade school with a Morty Arthur. But surely the dead man was not Morty? He would be my age and the body I had seen, while a little age-indeterminate, was not seventy-four, certainly. Apparently, however, the dead man was Morty's son, Willie Arthur. Was it at all possible that I might know Morty's son, Willie? I haven't set eyes on Morty in more than sixty years, I said--after we moved out of the neighborhood to a new place, at which time I started a new school in the seventh grade. And I never saw him again, ever. OK. Just a weird coincidence then? You bet weird. Well--very weird, but a coincidence absolutely. No way Willie could have known who you were from his father? Not that I know of, I said, stammering a little by now, admittedly shaken that there was even this slight connection. I mean, there was no connection at all. But as I said this, I was beginning to know it was a lie. I said it nevertheless thinking I would sort it out later. After a few more comments, Terrance said, OK, for now. That's all I need and you are definitely not to worry. Nothing to worry about at all. Perfectly innocent coincidence.

But he knew and I knew that the cops don't believe in coincidences. They now had a connection and would chew on it like terriers. They like "connections" that they can consider "leads" in a case. I don't watch ID, the murder channel, for nothing. So oh my goodness. Willie Arthur, shot and turning up in my potting shed, the shed of a woman who had gone to school with his father more than sixty years ago in a little elementary school on the upper west side of Manhattan. Good God. And what I didn't tell Terrance was that in fact I did have a contact with Morty Arthur a long time after that. I hadn't seen him, so I didn't lie, but I had talked to him on the telephone, twice, maybe forty years ago or more.

I had been in my office at the college. I have no idea exactly when this was, no context in which to place it, when I got a telephone call from a man who identified himself as Mortimer Arthur. I am guessing that I was maybe in my late twenties or early thirties when I got this call--just based on a few inexact external details. He said he had been in touch with my mother, located her in the phone book, and that she gave him my number. I remember at the time thinking it odd that my mother would give him my work number, but didn't think that impossible. I also thought it odd that out of the clear blue nowhere Morty would have a sudden urge to "reconnect," even though we hadn't ever been particularly connected to begin with, and then, after I moved, not connected at all; but who ever knows why people take strolls down memory lane. I don't remember a thing about the conversation--a kind of what are you up to, long time no see kind of fumbling exchange, I think--but do remember thinking it uncomfortable and kind of weird, considering again that I hadn't laid eyes on Morty since I was eleven years old and had not been particularly good pals with him even then. He had been in my class for a few years, how many, I was unsure of. I saw him every day along with the 23 other kids who were also in my class. Really, I could barely remember what he looked like.

After we hung up, not a very long conversation as I recall, I called my mother and indeed, yes, she had given my number to that "nice" young man. Apparently she remembered him better that I had. My mother was like that. Everyone whom I had ever known in my life was by definition "nice," and how "nice" that they wanted to be in touch with me. Mother, I said, we really don't know. Morty could have grown up to be a serial killer. Oh no, she said. Not him. He was a lovely boy. Well, I said, I really have no desire to reconnect or connect at all, so no more info to Morty, OK? Mom was a little huffy, but she finally promised, no more info to Morty. Fortunately she had not given him my home phone on the argument that during the day, the place to reach me was at work--but of course he could have found that number out, I guess, now knowing my married name. Those were the pre-Google days, though, so perhaps not.

A while later, maybe a few weeks, he called again at my office, this time trying to set up a meeting--maybe we could get together for lunch and get caught up? But this time, I was having no more. I said no--politely, I think--but that I was married, had a family, a job, friends, a social life--was really quite busy--and maybe I implied there would be a bit of impropriety in a "meeting," I'm not sure. I think he maybe said he was a salesman and got down to my "neck of the woods" from time to time. I'm not sure of that. At any rate, he was good natured the whole time, and when the call ended, I don't think I felt threatened or intimidated--just mildly annoyed. And, as it turned out, I never heard from him again, for which I was grateful. I did dig out my sixth grade class photo from the depths of the garage sometime after that second call and identified Morty in the group, a tallish dark haired boy with pointy bangs and big poppy eyes. Oh right, I thought. Mortimer Arthur. Sure. And then I forgot about the whole stupid thing--for years and years. Until Terrance called and said Morty's name.

So, why didn't I tell all this to Terrance? I don't know. The memory was just reviving, vaguely, as we talked and it seemed like it was nothing, and probably a connection that couldn't or wouldn't be traced, two forty-year-old phone calls of which there was now surely no record? It would have been a lot to tell Terrance for no particular reason--and that it was so long ago, so insignificant, my mother now long dead and not around to testify--if she would even remember. Why bother? I mean it was basically a joke at the time, some oddball who called me. If Willie Arthur had even been born at that time, his father would hardly have told his little boy about calling an old classmate from grade school. Still. I hadn't been forthcoming to my own lawyer. Oh well, I'd think about it and maybe call Terrance back and fess up, tell him I "just" remembered the calls from Morty a million years ago after we spoke. Old people have bad memories, right?

And then I wondered if Morty were still alive, had been informed of the death of his son, and somehow made the connection to the lady who owned the potting shed as me, his little sixth grade non-buddy buddy who hadn't wanted to "reconnect" a million years ago when he called me. Oh my God. I thought about Googling Morty, but jumped, knowing that the police can take your computer and if they found that I had Googled Morty, they would lock me up. Evidence!

I resolved I would call Terrance back the next day and spill the story. It's not good to lie to the police--and certainly not good to lie to your lawyer, I thought. I'd just say that I had the phone call episode in the back of my mind but that it took a day to come clear. In reality, I have a memory like an elephant, but Terrance didn't have to know that. A little dottiness is not a bad thing.

But the next day came and went, and then the next, and I still hadn't called Terrance to tell him, until I knew I wasn't going to. Big mistake, perhaps, but we girls have to have our little secrets, don't we?

4

Time passed. Life happened. The discovery of the body got a few more headlines, the manner of death, one gunshot to the back, and identity of the corpse, William Arthur, having been eventually announced, and then the story moved to the back pages of the newspapers, and off television entirely. My name had not appeared at all in any of the stories I had read or seen on TV, although the location of the "murder house" was given numerous times thus still clearly identifying me to those who knew me and the location of my home. I had no more calls from Terrance or Detective Eggers. So I kept house, fed the cats, dined with friends, saw my man-friend Harry from time to time. Peaceful, normal. My nothing life, exactly as desired, seemed to have resumed. Whenever asked about the body, less and less frequently, I simply said, I know nothing more. And that was true. Nothing.

I enjoyed a delightful and raucous Thanksgiving dinner at Martha's house with her engaging and interesting family and then started to make plans for my Christmas visit to San Diego to stay with Jared and his family. Jared made my travel arrangements, limo to the airport and plane reservations, while I took care of sorting clothes for the visit to a different climate as well as making domestic arrangements for mail stoppage and cat care, and then did the ever-dreaded Christmas shopping. For Jared and his family, I shopped almost exclusively online, arranging to have the packages delivered to his home. I'd wrap them when I got there, a few days before Christmas. For local friends, I shopped at local stores and wrapped, planning to distribute my gifts before I left--same as every other year.

And then the phone calls started.

At first, I didn't think anything about them. I had stopped monitoring my calls as the corpse news faded away and I did not expect to hear from the press or Eggers any more. I got my usual share of the horribly annoying robot calls, sometimes hanging up before the pre-recorded messages could click in. So, when I got a few calls at somewhat odd times when the caller clicked off, I didn't particularly take notice. I just assumed it was a failed robot call. But then the hang-up calls became more frequent and more regular, fairly early in the morning, about 7:30 AM, and fairly late in the evening, about 10:00 PM and I knew this was no robot. One call came one night when I had just fallen asleep and I picked up the phone, and while still half awake, heard what I thought was someone breathing on the other end, a kind of raspy and labored breathing. Suddenly, I was fully awake and just sat up in bed, rigid, until I got a dial tone that signaled the end of the call. But still I sat there in bed, holding the phone, listening to the dial tone as if it would tell me something that I vitally needed to know. And what the dial tone told me was that these were no accidental missed calls, but a pattern of--what?--attack, harassment, veiled threats--I knew not. I eventually dialed star-69 and was told that the number that had just called mine was "unavailable." Of course it was.

The next morning I got up, uneasily going about my morning business, expecting the phone to ring every minute after 7:00 AM. Amidst my angst, I kept trying to think about whom to tell, whom to appeal to. The phone company? Terrance? I eventually told Martha when she called later that morning and she said, Oh my God. Change your number. The thought of that had occurred to me, but when I thought of all the people I'd have to inform--changing a number that I'd had for forty years (and making it unlisted), I wilted. Maybe, I said--but not yet. A whole heap of trouble and explanations lie down that path. Well, I guess, Martha agreed, but said I couldn't just do nothing, could I? Good question.

Serendipitously, perhaps, Terrance called later that same morning and I told him about the calls--especially about the heavy breathing one the night before--and he offered the same advice as Martha had. That's all the phone company will tell you, he said, and so I agreed to give that some thought--and would definitely do so if the calls continued much longer. Terrance said he had just called to tell me he had heard nothing further from Detective Eggers or anyone else about "the matter." I told him I was going to see Jared in San Diego for two weeks over Christmas and was that OK? He told me it was fine, to have a great time, regards to Jared, and that he had all the contact information he needed in case anything should arise. He didn't say what that "anything" might be, and I didn't ask. Ignorance, bliss.

So, I flew off to San Diego a few weeks later, traveling light, basic wardrobe, but also with some stocking stuffers and Christmas wrap for the gifts that awaited me at Jared's. The limo drive to the airport with my stone-silent driver was the usual traffic nightmare, even at 6:00 AM up the Jersey Turnpike, and equally as aggravating was the check-in at the airport. Even with the curbside x-ray check-in for my bags, done slowly by a sleepy porter, there was a long line at the ticket counter, people in roped aisles moving like molasses, harried clerks in their spiffy blue uniforms, pounding away at computer keyboards and waiting, waiting--system is slow today (and every day!)--flipping tickets and boarding passes into envelopes and then chirping, "I can take whose next" to the maddened crowd.

And then the inevitable wait at the departures check point. When I finally got to the pass through, I kept setting off the beeper until I remembered my dental implants--could they be the culprits? So, of course, I had to go into the little booth with the lady agent, getting embarrassingly searched, and then having to open my mouth very wide to point out the three-tooth bridge implanted way back in my lower jaw. Seemingly satisfied, the lady agent, a bossy-pants type, took me back out and announced I was cleared to board. Like that was going to happen anytime soon, I thought, as I still had over an hour to flight time. But it was the only peaceful hour in the otherwise crazed morning. I poked around in a few gift shops, bought a book in the drugstore, and then settled in at one of the food courts with a cup of coffee. I finally wandered to my departure gate and awaited the boarding call. The departure lounge was pretty crowded, but I managed to get a seat next to an "undesirable," a person of dubious character, judging from appearances--big male, pony tail, beard, leather pants and cape, tattoos, beads, and a kind of crazed eye that wandered away from its mate. After I sat, he noticed my book, started talking about it, and turned out to be a really interesting man, kind of a hipster, I guess you'd call him, but smart, well-read, an interesting stranger. Time passed quickly and the call for first-class passengers went out more quickly than I had expected. I got up and was surprised that my new buddy also got up to board. So we wandered on board together, selected seats in first class, and got settled. He did not sit next to me, for which I felt a small regret, but, no matter as I planned to read and then sleep on the flight. First class was sparsely populated, maybe only five or six of us, so everyone got to sit alone, except for one couple who sat together, and we all sort of spread ourselves out into the adjoining empty seat. Finally, my trip started to get nice. Mimosas were served--or just plain orange juice--with coffee and small breakfast croissants. I had taken a Xanax before leaving my house as I have an incurable fear of flying which only Xanax seems to address. And as I sat there with my mimosa, I found that I felt no fear at all. I even forgot completely about the body, Mortimer Arthur, Willie Arthur, the phone calls, and the whole motley mess that would soon be 35,000 feet below and, a few hours later, 3,000 miles behind me.

The flight was smooth, uneventful, and I did what I had planned to do, read until the Xanax and, I suppose, the Mimosa had their combined effect and I dozed off. I woke for lunch service a few hours later, and then after enjoying an avocado salad, I prepared for landing in Denver and getting the connecting flight to San Diego. The landing was smooth, the transfer easy, only about a 30-minute wait, and I was soon settled in the new aircraft for the last leg of the flight. I noticed my bearded friend had also made the same transfer as I had, so he was San Diego-bound, too. We flew on over the Rockies and before I knew it, we were making another smooth landing, were being thanked for being aboard, were being told the local time, 11:32 AM, and the ground temperature, sixty-eight degrees, and I was getting my stuff together, stretching my stiff back, and making my way down the aisle and out of the plane, in front of my bearded and caped departure-lounge companion, still here. As we walked down the arrivals ramp, he asked if I was being met and I told him that I thought my son or daughter-in-law or maybe both would be there to get me. Just then, we entered the arrivals lounge and I spotted Jared among those greeting arriving passengers. He got to me, gave me a big hug, and then surprisingly greeted my bearded acquaintance who still stood behind me. Well, hello, he said to the man, Timmy Mooks, as I live and breathe. I was taken aback. You know each other, I asked Jared, with minor amazement. Yeah, Jared said, a little uncomfortably I thought, and then added, yes, sort of. Mr. Beard, now aka Timmy Mooks, just smiled, nodded, and then kept going, saying something like, see you around over his shoulder as he moved on.

So, that was weird, I said. Yeah, Jared said. He's a neighbor, a fairly new neighbor, kind of spooking the neighborhood with the beard and tats and leather stuff, but seems like an OK guy, even given his odd looks. Oh, I said, I thought that was sort of a California look, no? Maybe, Jared said, but not in my neighborhood where we tend to think Timmy has a sort of New York look, no offence. We both laughed at this counter coastal stereotyping, and moved on to the luggage arrival ports to wait for my single case.

Predictably, it was among the last to appear, so the arrivals lounge had pretty well cleared as we headed to the sidewalk where Lucy waited in the car, double-parked, their younger son Jack in the backseat, both waving and shouting hello to me. Oddly, we encountered Timmy Mooks again, standing on the sidewalk. As Jared got my case and carry-on into the trunk of the car and I hugged Jack through the car window, I noticed Timmy approach Jared and then, as both came around the car, heard Jared offer Timmy a ride home. Hate to impose, Timmy was saying apologetically, don't know what happened to my driver, supposed to meet my flight. No problem, Jared was saying, hop in. So Timmy and Jack and I arranged ourselves in the back of Jared's Mercedes, while Jared got in front, and Lucy pulled away into the steady stream of airport traffic and then out onto North Harbor Drive.

My daughter-in-law Lucy is an attractive woman. Without being conventionally pretty, she has tremendous style and one of those engagingly lethargic manners that constantly reassures you that everything's all right, nothing is trouble, she's good, we're good, it's a great day. She's a little above average height but seems tall as she is beautifully thin without being skinny. Her hair is streaky blond, just above shoulder length, always some version of the very simple bob she has worn her entire adult life. She has straight brows and arresting green eyes, her nose a bit small and her mouth slightly large, one of those slash mouths that is best when mobile--smiling or talking. Once encountered, she is remembered--for her very clean looks but more for her ease. She is one of those people who is at home with themselves, and I like her immensely. Today she is looking very Lucy with her beige slacks, beige and white striped cashmere top, gold earrings and big gold watch, pale orange lips, glossy and smiling, chatting to me from the driver's seat like a nonchalant tourist guide, pointing out some new additions to the landscape since I last visited. We are driving west to their home in La Playa--as I understand it, a neighborhood in the Point Loma area, across the bay from part of the large Naval installation that has defined San Diego for years as a Navy town. I have always found the geography of San Diego confusing, as is the case for any casual visitor to a strange city, but bordering on the Pacific and wrapped around San Diego Bay, with Coronado plunked in the middle of the Bay has always made it somewhat confusing for me. I'm never quite sure what water or land I'm looking at, never quite oriented. And as most east coast people, I am perpetually confused by having the ocean to the west rather than the east.

No one has yet mentioned "the body" or my recent related adventure because, I think, of Timmy Mooks' presence in the car. Somehow, I guess, this body, murder, has been classified as family business, not to be mentioned outside the family. Whatever, Jack is telling me about his winning soccer team and Lucy continues to interrupt with tourist information until we approach their house along Rosencrans Street. We stop a few doors before it to let Timmy Mooks out at his home, an impressive Spanish style villa on a generous lot, settled within huge palms and flowering beds. Lovely, I say, as Timmy grunts his thanks for the ride, grabs his bag, and wanders off up his winding drive toward the house. Big place, I say. Does he have family? Lucy tells me no, he seems to live there alone, a very old house, desperately in need of a thousand renovations so he probably got it at a good price, but doesn't seem to have done any work so far. But he's only been there for three or four months and he travels a lot, Lucy adds. I ask what line of work he's in, but Lucy says no one knows, a sort of mystery man.

We stop talking about Timmy as we pull into Jared's driveway a minute later, the drive leading up to Jared's house, more modest than Timmy's, on a smaller lot, but a lovely house, too. It is what we used to call modern but what they are now calling "mid century" modern, geometric lines, minimalist, wood stained driftwood gray, a bit stark but for the many grasses and shrubs used to landscape and soften the edges. I am vaguely reminded of the new house being built next to mine back home, but I shake that off, willing away memories of the past few months with all their dire implications. Jared and Lucy bought their house while Jared was still in the Navy, stationed in San Diego, and have spent years doing the renovations the house required--which is mainly what made it affordable for them. The house is on an elevated piece of land and so affords lovely views of the Bay and of downtown San Diego when, lit at night, is like a city-fairyland hovering over the water. The house is positioned to take full advantage of the views so that many rooms have a look at the Bay. As we all pile out of the car and gather my stuff, I am reminded as ever that San Diego has the perfect climate. It rarely gets below sixty or above eighty degrees, and while the residents find things to complain about, the low humidity or the Santa Ana winds, it is like Paradise to me.

We get me and all my things into the guest bedroom

where I spend the next half hour or so unpacking clothes and organizing all the little bags full of toiletries, my pills, my jewelry. The gifts I have had delivered sit in one corner, still in their delivery boxes, waiting to be opened and then wrapped. I hear Lucy moving around in the kitchen, calling to me to come have some coffee, and finally I feel settled enough to join her in the bright grey and white kitchen, immaculate with its shiny white cabinets, white marble counters streaked with grey veins, light grey walls, green growing things on window sills and hanging from rafters, a thoroughly clean, practical and comfortable kitchen that I have always enjoyed sitting in and sharing coffee and chatter with Lucy. She tells me "the guys" have gone to pick up lunch, so sit, have a coffee, and tell me all about this ghastly business with the body. We have spoken about it on the phone, but I now elaborate more, perched on my stool at the counter, leaving out some of the gory details, but telling her about the odd connection between my past and the body. I elect not to tell her about the two phone calls from Morty. I am working on repressing those memories. But I do tell her about the grade school connection and how weird it is that his son was the body. Spooky, is what Lucy says, and she's right. But let's talk about more pleasant matters--and we're off on family gossip, health issues, and domestic chit chat. Lucy is always easy to talk with. Soon, Jared and Jack arrive, loaded with Mexican take-out, on which we feast happily for the next half hour or so, my slim lunch on the plane forgotten in the face of crispy beef tacos, a favorite--although disdained by Jared in favor of more exotic and authentic Mexican fare--as he points out, referring to my plebian tastes. We are interrupted from our discussion of "authentic" food by a phone call which Jared takes and then returns to the kitchen looking slightly bemused. Well, that was our neighbor, Mr. Timmy Mooks, inviting us for drinks tonight to thank us for the ride. What did you tell him, Lucy asks, and Jared says he told Timmy he would call him back after checking with us--not sure of plans since I had just arrived and all that. Lucy thinks a bit and then says, well, we have no specific plans yet--and I would dearly love to see the inside of that wreck of a villa--but it's up to Mom, really. What do you think, she asks me. Are you tired--or do you want to see Timmy again?

I kind of smile and say that I don't really care, either way, as long as we can make it one drink and not some long, drawn-out party. Well, Timmy said five-thirty, says Jared, so that clearly sounds like a one-drink thing. OK with me, then, I answer, and so Jared goes off to call back and confirm our date with the mysterious Mr. Mooks.

5

I wake up sweating and frightened. I have dreamt something awful but I'm not quite sure what it was until the face of the body in the shed flashes into my head and I struggle to come fully awake and understand where I am and what is happening. I force myself to think rationally: I am in San Diego, at Jared and Lucy's and I am napping on the guest room bed. The face is of a dead man I discovered. I am having PTSD. The last thought alarms me most as I have never quite attributed any of my recollections about the body-find to a mental disorder. Is this possible? Am I having those notorious flashbacks and nightmares? Am I like a war veteran, battle-scarred and traumatized?

As I become more and more awake, I get calmer. I glance out the window and see the peaceful bay out there in the distance, shunting flashes of light from the sun off its little ripples. I hear the faint sound of voices coming from somewhere in the house, floating up to me and providing a peaceful reassurance. All is well. I stretch and arch my back and slowly roll over in preparation for getting up. There is something I must do. What is it? Oh yes. I must get ready to go to the neighbor's for drinks, to the house of my erstwhile traveling companion, the mysterious Mister Mooks. I stretch again and think about what to wear. I look down at my rumpled clothing and decide that a change is definitely in order. My sweater smells faintly of jet fuel.

I do a few stretch exercises that I learned in physical therapy as I lay prone in deference to my back, my stenosis, the stretches a hopeful guard against the sometime-pain I feel upon arising. I then put my knees together, pull them up toward my chest, roll to my side, and pull myself up slowly to a sitting position. I let my feet dangle for a while as I sit on the side of the bed, and then slowly stand, relieved to feel no significant back pain. If I can get out of bed without pain, I'm usually good to go. If not, it's more stretches and sometimes my back brace and anti-inflammatory pills.

I check my watch and see that it is almost five, just as I hear Lucy outside the bedroom door, softly tapping and calling to me. I open the door and tell her I'm up--just need to change clothes and will be ready shortly. She smiles, tells me I look fine--but I say I smell of airplane, but I'll be quick. I sponge my face, repair makeup, tease up my wilted hair, and put on a change of slacks and a top quickly and then locate Jared and Lucy in the kitchen, all spruced up and ready to go. Can we walk, Jared asks? Yes--I say--good for my back to get in some walking, and so off we go.

As we walk up Mr. Mooks' curved driveway, I notice more specifically what Lucy referred to as the shabbiness of the villa. The cream-colored stucco is peeling in many places, driveway pavers popping up here and there; a few roof tiles are missing, some shutters are crooked, and the gardens are in serious need of pruning and clearing. Some lovely japonica are blooming and their fragrance is sweet--but in a way, the sweetness of the flowers' aroma just adds to the sense of decadence one feels in approaching Mr. Mooks' front door. Before we reach the door, Mr. Mooks' opens it and stands there gesturing us in, a half-full cocktail glass in hand, obviously not having waited for us to start his cocktail hour. He looks reasonably conservative. The beard and pony tail seem groomed and he is dressed in dark slacks and a white gaucho shirt, neatly pressed. He is also wearing glasses which, oddly, seem to control his roving eye. Hello, hello he greets us and ushers us into a large foyer, sparsely furnished. There is an antique chest set below a gilt-framed mirror and, to the side of a curving staircase, I am moderately surprised to see a tall, fully decorated Christmas tree--all silver ornaments and white lights with even a few presents stacked underneath. The foyer seems immaculately clean, shining tile floors and dust-free surfaces. This environment prevails throughout the house, spare and immaculate, not cobwebby and dusty and falling apart as I think Lucy might have been expecting.

We move behind Mr. Mooks--call me Timmy--into a spacious room to the right of the foyer. The architecture continues to be Spanish, with red tile floors and decorative moldings and wall panels. But the furnishings are distinctly modern and minimalist in varying shades of grey with white and black accents. One dazzling Turkey rug with a predominant cerulean design sits in front of the fireplace on the right wall, lending the only splash of color to the room. At the far end, there is a line of French doors, opening on to a garden that, like the house's front garden, is in serious need of a gardener's attention. Also at that end of the room, to the right, is an elaborately carved oak bar where Timmy has taken himself to receive drink orders. I ask for my usual cocktail fare, a very sweet Manhattan, while Lucy and Jared opt for vodka martinis, up for Jared, on the rocks for Lucy, all with twists.

As we look around and politely compliment the beauty of some of the room's features, Timmy waves a hand nonchalantly and says, vaguely, thank you, much to be done, much work to be done. We make no comment on the various exterior signs of dishabille, but have quietly internalized the room's clean and orderly condition, the contrast between the inside and outside of the villa, and have moved on to other subjects. Timmy recalls the book I had been reading at the airport and says he knows the author's agent and that the author is a tedious and hermetic person in reality, impossible to work with. Really, I say. And yet her writing is so amiable! I know, Timmy says. I love her books. We talk more about a few of them and discover that we share the same favorite.

So, are you affiliated with the publishing trades, I ask? A leading question I know and don't care. Timmy smiles indulgently and says, no, no, not at all, and goes on to say rather vaguely something about international consulting. I feel I would be pushing the envelope to ask what the hell that means, but Jared picks up on that and guides the conversation to world travel and we all contribute little anecdotes about places we've been and sights we've seen and amazing travel experiences we've had, a perfectly dull little travelogue conversation, revealing little more about the ever-more mysterious Timmy. Although at one point I'm alerted to a reference Timmy makes to Inverness. Oh, I interject, my mother was born in Scotland, in Edinburgh, not up in

Inverness. And I notice Timmy rapidly changes the subject, as though he doesn't want to have to talk about Scotland. This is possibly imagined on my part.

And so cocktail hour moves along, desultory talk, superficial but pleasant, and Timmy proves to be a congenial host. I excuse myself to use the bathroom, pointed in the bathroom's direction by Timmy, and discover a perfectly ordinary little two-piece guest bathroom at the end of a hall off the entrance foyer, immaculately clean and stocked with paper hand towels on a little glass shelf above the sink. I notice a large dining room off to my left as I make my way to the bathroom, a dining room furnished with a parson's table and six chairs, a bland silk flower arrangement placed in the center of the table, and a long low cabinet on one side of this sparsely furnished and immaculately clean room. When I finish in the bathroom, I return to the others and resume conversation. At one point, Timmy produces a tray of snacks, rather elegant for this single male world-traveler to have prepared on his own--and I wonder if there is a maid or a lady-love in his life when he dispels the mystery by telling us about *Canapés a Go-Go*, a new online food service and his source for the snack platter. Jared accepts a half refill for his martini while Lucy and I decline; we all munch on the canapés, and eventually, after a little more than an hour, the visit draws to a close as Lucy remembers a casserole she has in the oven for our dinner--and Jared refuses any more drinks refills. Timmy smiles, rises unceremoniously, and sees us to the door, thanking us again for the ride from the airport. I remark on the beauty of his Christmas tree on the way out, but he reveals nothing about his Christmas plans or for whom the wrapped presents might be intended. As he closes the door he says, come back, don't be strangers and we all wave fingers in his direction and say, of course, but by then the door is shut and Mr. Timmy Mooks has retired back into his confusingly shabby, elegant villa.

So, I say, as we walk back down the drive, pleasant enough, your mysterious international consultant neighbor Mr. Mooks, wouldn't you say? And Jared says CIA. And Lucy and I both say CIA what? Or some other kind of intelligence spook, Jared goes on. Whoa, I say: Mr. Mooks is a spy? Well, said Jared, you can never be certain with these guys--but all that warehoused furniture that they move in and out of safe houses, and many of the places he spoke about related to his travels that all have some kind of intelligence implications. I don't know. The only odd thing is why he would invite us over. If he is a spook, he would know that I used to be in Naval Intelligence and so might nose him out. And, these guys usually play it close, rarely socialize locally or invite an inspection of their personal lives--or, in his case, lack thereof. Jared pauses. Well, there were the tree and the presents, I said. All staged, Jared answered.

We walk on in silence, Jared offering no more speculation, Lucy checking her watch with thoughts drifting back to the dinner casserole, and me chasing some kind of elusive idea working itself out in some part of my mind that I can't quite access. And all of this goes poof as we approach the house and see a car in the driveway. Oh, Lord, says Lucy, Grant is home! How perfect! And so he is. Grant the older son appears in the doorway, hails us and runs down to meet us--handshake with Jared, hugs for Lucy and me. You're here early, Lucy exhales, and Grant laughs and says my little surprise, got to take my last final early so I could get here to see grams--and he hugs me again. What a sweetheart, I say. I have always called him my sweetheart, even now that he is a six foot four, twenty year old college junior--still my little sweetheart. In a minute, Jack runs out to join us and we all walk arm in arm, back into the house.

In the warmth of Grant's early arrival and our dinner talk and eating a delicious cheesy tomato pasta casserole with a crisp green salad accompaniment, Timmy and the strange visit to the villa are quickly forgotten and a reunited family basks in that warm glow for the rest of the evening. We top off our cozy time watching the last half of Monday Night football and because I am on the west coast, I am able to stay awake to watch the whole game for a change. Grant has updated me on his junior year and Jack has related some funny stories arising from his role on his high school soccer team, not a staring role at all, according to him. Jack is a bit of a natural comedian, is cute as he relates self-deprecatory stories about poor performances and embarrassing moments in his soccer career but is proud of the team's success nonetheless.

As I finally retire, tired from my long day, regardless of my afternoon nap, I think that I will wrap my presents in the morning when it will be Christmas Eve day already! I think again of our visit to Timmy Mooks and keep grabbing at that thought, still trying to surface. I think of Jared's observation that Mooks could be a spy and for some reason, this activates that gnawing thought which finally surfaces and somehow connects with Morty Arthur and the body of his son in my shed. What could these have to do with each other? Why has my mind signaled a connection? Maybe it's just the quality of mystery both share. Maybe it's also the sense that Timmy being on my flight was perhaps not in fact a coincidence. It seems almost too pat, too easy--the same flight, the absent transport from the airport. Who was it who said that there are no coincidences in life? And then what about all those years that Jared spent in Naval Intelligence in Maryland before his final duty assignment in San Diego? What mysteries, big secrets with international implications could he know? Suddenly I seem wrapped up in something huge and unknowable with forces I could not even recognize--murder, spying, international consulting. And suddenly my head starts to spin and I am not tired at all. I am awake, alert--and I am afraid.

But the next morning, after a surprisingly sound and dreamless sleep that I was finally able to drift into, things shift back to normal. Breakfast, coffee, chatter, the two boys still sleeping, then me ensconced in my room, wrapping up a storm, everything comes back into balance and the mysterious shroud that enveloped me the night before has dispersed, gone in the glorious morning sunshine. Later in the day, I receive a surprising phone call from Terrance Hannity, my lawyer. He says he has no news of any kind related to "the case," just wants to convey holiday wishes to me and to Jared and Lucy. He asks casually if I'd had a good flight and Timmy's image briefly jumps to my mind, but I say oh yes, very smooth, slept much of the way. He seems about to follow up, but then brings the call to an end by repeating his holiday wishes and then hanging up. I think the call odd, but say nothing. Jared had spoken to him for several minutes before handing the phone to me, and I'm not sure what they were talking about. In fact, Terrance had done most of the talking, with Jared just saying uh-huh and sure and fine--a very one-sided chat. I thought to ask Jared what Terrance had to say, but decided not to be a nosey nanny, and didn't.

6

I'm back in New Jersey, headed south out of Newark Airport, down the Turnpike to the Garden State Parkway, homeward bound. My driver this time is chatty, asking me if I had a nice trip, how was the weather, why do we all live in New Jersey when we could live in a paradise climate like southern California, and on and on. I am tired and probably not the conversationalist I should be, and eventually the chatter subsides and I am left to my thoughts--mostly memories of the past two weeks, even more especially golden as I look out at the snow-covered landscape that is New Jersey in January.

It had been a glorious two weeks, a delightful Christmas day with way too many presents, a turkey dinner with all the trimmings at home for the five of us, and then days of touring and shopping and dining out and, especially good, my annual visit to the amazing San Diego Zoo, one of my most favorite places in the world. We had a lovely New Year's eve dinner at a restaurant called Nine-Ten up in La Jolla with two other couples, welcoming in the new year with champagne and chic noise makers. And then one night near the end of my visit, Lucy had a casual party, inviting a group of their friends whom I had come to know over the years and it was pleasant seeing everyone and getting caught up on their news. Oddly, at the last minute, Lucy thought it might be nice to invite Timmy Mooks to the party, to introduce him to some of the friends who were also neighbors, but she got no response to her calls and there was no answering machine on which to leave a message, so he was not at the party for which I was inordinately thankful for reasons I didn't dwell on.

After the party and clean up were over, I retired, rather late, probably near midnight, and spent some time winding down, getting ready for bed, watching a little TV, stretching out some aches and pains. Finally, I felt settled and ready to sleep, so I turned off the lights and the television and wandered over to the window to catch a look at the bay and the city lights. As I looked out, I noticed a car driving slowly past the house, and as it passed under a streetlight, I caught a glimpse of the driver. I only saw him for a few seconds and hardly paid much attention until I suffered a slight shock and stopped as if frozen on my way to the bed. The man driving had been a shaved, besuited, and short-haired version of Timmy Mooks, I was sure of it. I turned back to the window, but of course the car was gone, it's tail lights sketched as two pale red dots down the night street. But I was as sure as I could be, even with only two seconds of vision and three seconds of mental recognition, that a spiffy and conventional Timmy had just driven by Jared's house at 12:42. What the hell, I thought? What the hell.

I mentioned this at breakfast the next morning. Jared had already left for work and Lucy humored me as best she could, but clearly thought I had been mistaken--and I decided not to insist, simply saying she was probably right, that I was imagining things. But I was not.

And so that was what I was thinking of the most as my chatty driver, now silent, drove me down the Garden State Parkway and back to my home, the murder house, scene of the crime and my ghastly discovery. Welcome back.

After an uneventful drive, home by 8:30 PM, and after tipping and saying good-bye to my driver--too chatty, but a pleasant man who helped me in with my bags--I flop on a chair in the breakfast room and think of what I have to do. It is too late to retrieve the cats from the kennel, so that would wait until tomorrow morning. I can't face the task of unpacking everything, but think I should at least unpack the carry-on bag that holds my toiletries, some of which I'll need before bedtime. I go into the guest room where I'd had my driver deposit my bags and I unzip my carry-on. It holds all my toiletries plus a few of the smaller Christmas gifts that I'd stuffed in spare spaces. As I take items from the bag, I notice a small package, still wrapped in gold and white paper. Bemused, I pick it up and wonder how I had missed opening this little package--and, more, how it, still wrapped, has come to be in the bag, a bag that I had packed myself. The gift has no tag of any sort. It occurs to me that perhaps Jared or Lucy or one of the boys had slipped it into the carry-on to give me a further little surprise after I got home, which seems very sweet to me. I take off the wrapping to find a small blue box, the size that might hold a bracelet or brooch--unmistakably a Tiffany box. I open it and remove the flat cotton pad on top and then nearly drop the box and let out a yelp, because what is nestled in the cotton pad on the bottom of the box is a bullet.

I don't know bullets--their size, caliber, the gun for which they are intended, nothing. This one is brass and gold and rather pointy and looks like maybe what I would call a medium sized bullet, this assessment based strictly on my view of them on my crime shows on television. I look at it, my hand shaking as I hold the box, but some little voice says don't touch it, don't remove it, put the cotton back on top, close the box, and think, really think, what to do. I set the closed box on the dresser, retrieve the wrapping and set it next to the box, and then sit down on the bedroom chair because my knees as well as my hands are shaking. I know I should call the police but then immediately know I shouldn't. I should call Terrance Hannity, but instead I just sit there. I am thinking that Mafia people send bullets to people as warnings--hadn't I read that in a crime novel somewhere? Is this a threat? The body in the shed, the Mafia, are they connected? How could I be a threat? Why would someone send me this "message," if that's what it is--and how in the hell did it get into my carry-on bag? Who put it there? Who had access?

I don't know how long I sit there until I finally get up, go into the dining room, take out the bottle of scotch, untouched since the police had me drink it weeks ago, and pour a little into a lovely crystal glass from a set I rarely use. Fine thin glass, I think irrelevantly, thick ornate base. The set was a gift from a Swedish friend. Swedish glass. Why am I thinking that? I sip slowly and because no useful thoughts come to me as my throat burns from the alcohol, I just decide to do absolutely nothing at all. My mother used to tell me: When in doubt, do nothing--better no act than a bad act. So I just sit there and sip the scotch, which is about as nothing as I can do at the moment.

Eventually I get up and wander back into the guest room, vaguely focused on doing what I had started to do--unpack my toiletries from my carry-on, put the pajamas that I wore my final night in San Diego into the dirty clothes hamper, unzip my large suitcase and take out the few garments that I had packed on their hangers--and put them in the closet. I start to do this in a rather mechanical and unthinking way until I am seized with a panicky notion. I feel that I must go out into my dark and cold and snow covered garden and make my way to the shed and go stand inside of it. This is more than an urge. It is a compulsion, and before I know it, I am through the sun room, out the doors, across the big back deck, and trotting through the snow in the direction of the shed.

I am freezing in just my slacks and sweater, no coat, and I am telling myself how irrational this behavior is, but I go on anyway. When I am about fifty feet from the shed, I stop suddenly. I am aware, somehow, that I am not alone. I move quietly behind a huge oak tree to my left and just stand there, my hand on the tree's cold trunk, motionless, breathing softly, aware, aware, very still. Cautiously, I look around the tree in the direction of the shed, and there, someone is moving, I can see him--or his outline etched against the snowy ground. Inadvertently, I let out a sound--a kind of groan of fear and surprise over which I have no control whatsoever. The figure by the shed stops still. And then I turn and with energy derived from my panic, I race back across the garden, up onto the deck, through the doors still ajar, and into my sun room. I push the doors closed hard behind me, lock them, and then lean against them breathing hard and fast. I finally sit on the couch in the sun room, afraid to move, afraid to look out. But when I finally do look through the glass of the French doors, the moon shines down on my snowy yard and I see nothing, nothing but snow and trees and the potting shed in the distance, innocently guarding its secrets.

7

The next morning I finish unpacking, consciously ignoring the little bullet nestled in its little blue box sitting atop my dresser. I put my Christmas presents away, return my shoes and slightly worn garments to my closet, sort things for the wash, and take my travel bags back out to the garage, humping them up onto the storage shelves from whence they came. I wash and dress and return to my breakfast room for another cup of coffee. I make a list of errands for the day, on top of which is retrieving my cats from the kennel, a place called Purr n' Pup, which they hate, for which I don't blame them. Kitty prison. My heart always aches when I drop them off, which is not often, but I have no choice, I tell myself. I just worry too much that the in-home cat minders will somehow inadvertently let them out and that they will die out there in a world with which they are totally unfamiliar.

Once my to-do list is made, I have little else to think about and so the bullet comes back to my mind and the questions remain: Who put it there, how, when, and why. I try to think about when my bags were out of my sight, who had access--but these thoughts are dead ends. The only answers are my family and the airline baggage handlers, and these seem like doubtful culprits. So I purposefully walk back into the guest room, open the top drawer of the dresser, empty but for a few boxes of seldom-worn jewelry, and put both the blue box and its Christmas wrapping into that drawer. Out of sight, out of mind. That is my approach for now. I will think about it later. Or not.

I am busy for the rest of the day. I am so happy to have my little furry creatures back who both run around the house in delight after I let them out of the carry case and then go directly to their food which I have already fixed for them. I do my food shopping, go to the post office to pick up my mail, call Martha, text a few other friends, confirm a few dates, and do my room-by-room house cleaning. By four, I am tired, although it is just 1:00 PM west coast time--which I have gotten used to--and so I shouldn't be tired. Jet lag, maybe. I drain the remainder of the coffee pot into my mug, heat it up in the microwave, flop in an easy chair, sip my coffee, and let myself think about the prowler from the previous night. Two criminal things--the bullet and the prowler--both of which I know I should report--or should have reported--to the police, and would have done so immediately were it not for what the police have come to mean since the body dump. Always a believer in the grade school mantra, *the policeman is your friend*, I have all my life relied upon and called upon the police in times of need. But now, I am fearful. How can I call on them when my lawyer has told me not to talk with them further. The implication is that they are not to be trusted, that I am a person of interest in a murder, and that any action on my part may increase my exposure. My world is upside down.

Finally, about 4:30, I place a call to Terrance Hannity, determined to tell him everything and seek his counsel. But he is out of the office for the week, I am told. There is someone covering for him with whom I could speak, but I decline the invite and just leave a call-back request, whenever convenient. So there, I tried, I think. And then turn my thoughts toward domestic things, daily plans.

A few nights later, I am out for dinner with my friend of many years, Harry. My boyfriend, I guess, although our erstwhile romance has simmered into a lovely friendship, companionship, mutually supportive and comforting. It is one of the pleasures of old age. When romance dissolves, closeness increases. I am debating whether or not to tell Harry about the recent developments--the bullet, the prowler--since my return from San Diego. Terrance has not yet called back, a delay that I expected since I did not add a note of urgency to my request for a call back. I am looking at Harry, a tall man with good posture, silver hair, still-bright blue eyes and am really tempted to just indulge myself and tell him everything. But caution has overwhelmed me. What if somehow this information becomes incriminating and, by telling Harry, I somehow involve him or, worse, make him a witness against me for knowing something I did not tell the police. I think, vaguely, that I watch too many TV crime dramas and have become paranoid as a result. Still.

The restaurant is lovely, low lighting, white tablecloths, fine china and silverware, a harpist playing softly on the other side of the room. The food is delicious--I have just finished sharing Oysters Rockefeller with Harry--and our cocktails are crisp and cold. Why drag my frightening news--my fear itself--into this otherwise pleasant evening? It's an interlude, I tell myself. It's a night away from my fear, my uncertainty. I don't want to sully this night. I just want to drift on my cloud of pleasure and peace. So I say nothing, have another sip of my drink, and talk of pleasant things--my grandsons, the sights of San Diego, the paradisiacal weather there, anything that does not remind me of my terror.

Harry and I get back to my house about ten after our steaks and then *crème brulet* have been consumed and he declines my offer to come in and have a nightcap. He's had enough to drink, he says, and really so have I. He gives me the customary hug and peck on the cheek, waits until I am in the house, and have re-set the alarm, and then drives off with his usual brief horn toot that always signals the end of our evenings out. But once inside, I am uneasy. I think back to the peculiar hang-up phone calls that were increasing in frequency before I left for California, but have not resumed since my return. Inevitably I think of the bullet, the prowler, Timmy Mooks, and my head feels as if it will explode. I pour myself a thimbleful of Drambuie, give the cats a few treats, close all the blinds and drapes, and prowl around my house slowly, restlessly. Pointlessly, I pick up the local weekly paper again and scrutinize every page, hoping for some little news story about my found body, but in vain. Nothing.

Finally, finally, I retire to my bedroom, my cats dutifully following me down the hall, ready to take their places on either side of my pillow and hunker down for a night of peaceful sleeping. Peaceful for them, but restless for me, filled with fragmented dreams, haunted and filled with phantasmal people, stalking me, blocking my passage down long familiar but unrecognizable passageways. I wake gasping, hear unfamiliar sounds in the garden, sit up, paralyzed by fear and then, after some deep breathing and pleasant imaging, I relax and miraculously fall back into a sounder and more dreamless sleep than I have known for months.

The next morning about ten, I get my call back from Terrance Hannity, my lawyer, and before I can decide what to say, I say it all--the calls from Morty Arthur forty years ago, Timmy Mooks, the bullet, the prowler. It's as if a damn burst inside my head and I am no longer in control of my speech. Terrance lets me go on and on without interrupting, lets me catch my breath, and then starts to slowly unravel my narrative with questions that attempt to create a chronology. He never once asks me why I haven't mentioned any of this before, attempts at one point to insert the mysterious phone calls which I had previously told him about into the time line he is developing, seems to be writing things down as I answer his queries, and stays as calm as if he and I were discussing the weather. So, that's all of it, he asks finally? Yes, I said. That's all of it. Surely that's enough to make him think he really is dealing with a lunatic--or a killer. All of it. Do we need to meet or talk further, I ask. Do I need to do anything? Not for now, Terrance tells me, but let me get back to you in a few days. Be sure your doors and windows are locked, your alarm set, and do not touch that bullet or its packaging. Leave it where it is for now. I'll call you Monday or Tuesday.

After I hang up, I feel surprisingly better, unburdened I guess. I feel freed up to do what I have been trying to do for weeks, live my normal, peaceful, happy, uneventful life, my murder-free life. Oh, God, let me do the nothing that I have been doing, the nothing that I love.

And I do manage that--well, almost--over the weekend. My banal existence is interrupted only once by yet another unexpected visit from my neighbors-to-be, this time by both Mariah and Tad together. They come late Saturday morning, both standing on my doorstep when I answer their knock, looking a little fidgety, but vibrant and stylish as ever. Tad is youthful looking, clean and scrubbed with his blond hair and red cheeks. He is in some ways a striking contrast to the hip, dramatic Mariah. He is the all-American boy in his pressed khaki's, low boots and a black, knee-length overcoat over a white turtleneck sweater. His teeth are as white as his sweater, his smile wide as he stretches out his hand and says so nice to see you again. Mariah is, as ever, dramatic, in black leggings, long black boots, and some kind of large faux fur jacket and matching hat.

I invite them into the breakfast room, sunny and bright on this clear and freezing morning, and let them shed their outerwear as I head to the kitchen for coffee, just black they have both said. We all settle over our mugs and I ask how the snowy weather is affecting the house construction. Tad tells me that there is a lot of interior work to be done which is moving forward, even with snow on the ground. I mention the expected thaw forecast for the next few days and Mariah smiles at me, her sooty eyes flicking around the room as if looking for something she misplaced. After exchanging more small talk, Tad says that the real reason for the visit is that he was wondering if I would consent to having a tree removed. It's technically on your property, he explains, but leans over onto ours and interferes with a border fence we are planning to install. I am rather protective of my trees and so ask him to go outside with me and point out which tree he is talking about. It turns out to be just an old pin oak and not the nearby ash tree that I prize, and so I say, shivering and anxious to go back inside, that removing the oak would not be a problem for me. Of course, he adds, we will pay. Yes, I respond. Good. Let's go back and finish our coffee.

Tad and Mariah seem pleased to have settled the tree issue so quickly and painlessly and seem anxious to be gone now that they've been polite and gotten their wish. They finish their coffee, don coats and hat, and we walk back to the door. Tad then asks, casually--too casually?--if I'd heard any more from the police about--he hesitates, looking for the right words--"that matter," he says finally, gesturing vaguely in the direction of my potting shed. I say no, not a word and then add that if I never hear about it again it would suit me just fine. Both Tad and Mariah agree, shaking their heads energetically as they take their leave. Thanks for the coffee--and for the tree thing. Probably won't come down for another few months. We'll let you know when.

And then they were gone, sweeping out into the cold air like two figures from a magazine cover.

8

I get a brief call from Terrance on Monday morning asking me if he might stop by my house the next afternoon. Yes, of course you can, I say, and we settle on a time. I didn't ask him why, but know I will fret until he gets here.

The next day, I busy myself with some menial chores, run down to the bakery to get some fancy cookies to offer Terrance with coffee that afternoon. I eat lunch, and then fuss a little, a very little, with hair and makeup in advance of his arrival.

In due time, he comes and I have a moment of *deja vu.* My mind goes back almost forty years to the days when Terry would come to our house to visit with Jared, Terrance a leggy, tall, teenage boy, blonde, freckled, smiling, polite, just the kind of friend one would want for one's son. In many ways, he has changed very little. His mature body is still tall and slender, and while the freckles are gone, his hair is still fair, his complexion rosy. He wears small, neat rimless glasses. Today, he wears a heavy parka over his grey business suit. The promised thaw has not yet arrived and the ground is still covered with patchy, dirty snow. The temperature remains well below freezing and the air is raw and damp.

Come in, come in and get warm, I say, as I probably would have said forty years ago. Different house, mature Terrance, same me.

We settle in the breakfast room. I bring in the coffee and a plate of the cookies and am relieved to see Terrance eat two--and then a third.--with the lost boy's delight. He comments on them and I tell him about the new bakery in town and about how good it is. But things don't stay cozy for long.

Terrance tells me that he has consulted with one of the law partners who specializes more directly with criminal law. They have apparently concluded that they need to revise my file to include, among other things, a chronology of my "association" with Mortimer Arthur. Terrance pauses here to ask me if I have ever, on any occasion, no matter when, had contact with his son William, the victim, even casually, or at a distance. No, I say. And then to make it sound legal add, categorically no. OK, good, he says. He goes on to say that he has had had two more calls over the past few months from Detective Eggers--he doesn't specify when or about what--but says he feels that the investigation is heating up and that he believes that I am a "person of interest." Now, he adds quickly, don't panic. This is, more or less, routine for an investigation--my house, my discovery of the body, my past history with the victim's father. Oh my God, I say and then Terrance pats my hand and says, it's OK, it's all right. I am trembling a little and say how on God's earth can this be. How could this crazy association with little Morty Arthur in grade school have such dire consequences? It's a nightmare.

Terrance goes on to ask about the hang-up phone calls. Have they resumed? No. How about the bullet? Still in my drawer. He then takes an envelope out of his briefcase, an envelope that looks like what you see police use on TV to collect "evidence." He asks me to take him to the bullet, so we go into the guest room where he removes it and its wrapping from my dresser drawer, and places these in the bag, sealing, signing and dating the seal. Just part of the file, he says, and smiles rather wanly. He asks if I have any idea of how it got into my suitcase and I tell him it was in my carry-on bag and that, no, the only people whom I thought could have had access were my family and the airline baggage handlers, neither of which seemed likely. And, besides, I had carried the bag onto the plane myself and stashed it in the overhead during the flight, left unobserved only during my trips to the ladies room. Was the bag locked? No, never. We go back to the breakfast room and have more coffee and more cookies for Terrance. I nibble on one myself, sweet, strawberry icing. And then he continues. He asks me a lot of questions, similar to those asked by Eggers--particularly about my "alibi" on the presumed day of the murder, about owning a firearm, and then has me go over again, in as much detail as I can remember, the calls from Morty those many years ago when my mother had put us "in touch." And you never saw him then? No, no, and no. Did you mention the calls to anyone, then or later? I don't know, I say. Except for my mother. But I don't remember whether or not I told anyone else or not--probably not. It was meaningless and something I just really forgot about quickly.

He moves on to ask questions about the prowler near the shed on the night of my return from San Diego. Did I recognize the person? No. Male or female? I assumed male--but now I can't say for sure. The person was crouched over, appeared to be wearing bulky outerwear, a big puffy coat or parka, and a wooly hat. It was too dark to see any more than an outline against the snow--and then fear took over and I fled. About what time of night? I think about that. I was home by 8:30, unpacked, found the bullet, had a drink. When? Maybe about 10:00 PM, I say. Maybe a little later? Is it possible that someone knew of your travel plans, thought you were still away and so felt free to trespass? I suppose so, I answer. I mean, I go to Jared's every year for Christmas and New Year, board my pets, stop my mail. My friends would all know, plus the gal in the Post Office and the people at the kennel. It's a small town. People generally know me and what I do.

We then move on to Timmy Mooks, the astounding coincidence of our same flight to San Diego, of our visit to his house, of Jared's observation that the guy was a spook--and then of my sighting of him from the bedroom window, driving past Jared's house on the night before my departure. I suggest that Terrance call Jared if he wants more on Mr. Mooks who is, after all, as far as I know, still Jared's neighbor--with or without the hair and the beard.

OK, he says, great, and seems to be finished. Then he adds, almost as if it were an afterthought, would you be willing to pay for some private investigation into the Arthurs, father and son? And maybe also Mr. Mooks? Much could be done online at minimal cost, but we may need to send out a guy to follow up if anything funny turns up. Yes, I say, sure, of course. But why? Well, he says, we have to start thinking about preparing a preliminary defense. Defense? I almost scream the word. Defense, I yell again. Terrance, you are kidding me right? Please tell me you are kidding me. Again, he pats my hand and says that they are just being overly cautious, staying on top of things, doing what they feel is in my best interests, covering all the bases, considering my exposure, and all the supposedly comforting jargon lawyers use to really say: *You could be in trouble.*

I get goose bumps. You hear this, that people get goose bumps, as metaphor, but I really did. I look at my arms and there are little bumps all over them. Terrance, I say, I am a high anxiety person, a Type A personality, and you're scaring me to death. He smiles. He tells me he is sorry and says, vaguely, some things just should be done. I am waiting for him to say he "had my back," but thank goodness he didn't. Had he done so, I might have thrown the rest of the cookies at him.

One thing, I say, as he is gathering his notes and getting up to leave, and I don't know if this matters. But it's about my new neighbors, the people building the big pile up the hill? He looks curious. I continue: Well, twice since the body arrived they have stopped by--first the wife, then both of them. Curiously, they had never really sought me out at home before. We had just chatted casually on the road or in the lane, but they made two purposeful visits after "the event." They had excuses for both--first, her concern over the body, property values, you know, probably legitimate concerns and just natural curiosity after such a grisly event. Then the next visit on Saturday was about a tree of mine they want to remove to make way for a boundary fence, also perfectly reasonable--and Tad, the husband, only referred to "the incident" as they were leaving, quite casually referred to it. And what did you tell them, Terrance asks. Nothing, I say. Nothing. Know nothing, saw nothing, have heard nothing. Nothing. What is their last name, he asks. Ummm--Mariah and Tad Something. I struggle. Washington? No, wait. Worthington. Mariah and Tad Worthington. Terrance dutifully jots this down, too. And then he continues to gather his things, patting his little stack of papers together, and putting them and the evidence bag into his brief case.

Finally, he leaves, dear sweet Terrance, that used-to-be gangly fair-haired freckled kid who has just thrown my head into a cacophony of jarring thoughts, dizzying, disturbing, thoughts that I would have to find new room for in my head before I could put them away.

9

On Friday I decide to go to the gym. The promised thaw has arrived, that lovely and rare mid-winter springtime that we are occasionally gifted by the gods. It is almost fifty degrees, a bright clear sunny day that feels new and energizing. I had joined the gym a few years before to take a chair yoga class twice a week, mainly because a few of my friends were doing the class and the temptation of sitting while exercising was moderately appealing. I actually enjoyed the classes, the lively instructor, and the ladies who took the classes with me--all older ladies, but very committed to the stretching and moving the classes required. And I was surprised at how much exercise we actually got. It was a bit of a misnomer--the chair part--as we spent half the time on our feet, but sort of using the chair to do various stretches and muscle pulls. It made me feel moderately virtuous and I loved the looks on the faces of my friends when I said I was going to or just got back from the gym. You? The gym? Seriously, their expressions said.

I even went to Walmart and bought a few gym clothes--long and knee-length stretchy pants, some colorful tank tops, and a weird-looking pair of sneakers with a wide toe expanse that let my toes move and breathe. I looked absurd in these get-ups, which served to show every lump and bump of fat on my old body, but I admitted that they were comfortable and sort of fit in with the outfits of the other gym goers. The gym culture was definable, from the clothes to the population. From early morning to about 8:00 AM, the crowd was young, career folks getting their hour in before work, strapping guys lifting big weights and skinny gals doing steps or running flat out on the treadmills. Then, from 8:00 until about noon, the population was markedly aged, often including folks with walkers or serious physical disabilities. The hours from about noon until 2:00 PM saw a smattering of the young professionals on lunch break and soccer moms whose kids were secure at school, their chores done in the morning. From then until about 4:00 PM, however, the gym was veritably empty. When I discovered this, I knew what time was good for me to go. I liked the empty feeling and having my choice of bikes and treadmills without having to wait for one to be free. So on the days I didn't take a class, I'd often go mid-afternoon for a little personal work-out: bike, rowing machine, treadmill, steps, arm weights, about 25 minutes total, all the boredom I could bear. I followed this routine, on again, off again, for almost a year--classes interspersed with work-out afternoons.

But then, as with all my forays into programmed exercise, I went less often, then not at all, then every so often, then again not at all. It had been months since I had been there, but I have been so restless and anxious since Terrance's visit that I suddenly think maybe a little body-in-motion time will be helpful.

So, I go. I'm not signed up for any class, so I just spend

some time on the stationary bike, the rowing machine, the treadmill, and then with the weights doing arm exercises I had learned when I went for back therapy. As I sit on the little leather bench, pumping iron--I laugh to myself as my five-pound weights hardly constitute iron or pumping--I spot someone in the mirror into which I am starting, a mirror that reflects the big gym behind me. It is a fleeting glance, someone familiar has caught my attention. I stare again and try to see the reflected image that has seemed familiar to me. I am thinking it is one of those men who questioned me at my house after I found the body, one of those undefined and never seen again people I just thought of as "detectives" and then forgot about. Was that who I saw? Was I being *followed*, my God? I persist with my weights and arm raises but have a huge bubble of anxiety rising in my chest, looking back into the mirror to prove myself right or wrong. There. He comes into view again, moving about thirty feet behind me onto some huge machine on which he sits, with his back to me. So he is now fully visible to me, but from his back I can tell nothing, just a medium built man of indeterminate age in a black tee. It could be him. And, if it is him, he could be here just to exercise, as it is a big gym with a large membership which could obviously include local cops.

Still. I start to sweat. I hardly ever exercise hard enough to break a sweat and am not doing so now with my little old lady weights and arm lifts. This is not muscle sweat. It is anxiety sweat. But I will finish my routine, go to the fountain for a drink of water, then go to the ladies locker room to retrieve my jacket--and then leave the gym. I will do as I always do. And when I do all this and return to the floor of the gym, moving toward the exit, the man I think is a cop following me is no longer sitting on the big machine and is nowhere that I can see as I casually look around. I return the locker key to the still-smiling girl at the front reception, get my car keys and gym ID from her, smile back and say thank you, and make my way out to the parking lot and then to my car. I get in, start the car, and then just sit there, breathing hard. I notice I am still sweating.

So much for going to the gym so that I can relax.

I stop at the drug store on the way home, all the time driving especially carefully, walking slowly around the drug store barely remembering what I came for, but looking always behind me or in the rear-view mirror when driving, to see if I can spot any one person or car that is there continuously. I see nothing like this. No one seems to have followed me into the drug store; no customer or clerk seems to be paying me any special attention. I feel like a character in a spy novel as I ponder which shampoo to buy, what vitamins I have run out of and need to replenish, what new shade of nail polish I want to try, all the time sneaking peeks to see who is watching me. No one. I chat casually with the cashier as I pay for my purchases and then leave the store. I continue to drive slowly home, check the road and the lane outside my house for any strange vehicles, and finally get into my garage and then my house without noticing anything untoward. Was it all my imagination, the guy in the gym? Just as I am beginning to relax and perhaps even retrieve the advantage gained from my exercise, I notice my message machine flashing and press the button to get a message from Terrance, asking me to call his office at my earliest convenience.

I don't want to call. I don't ever want to speak to Terrance again. I no longer even want to be me with this unbearable weight on my back, pushing, pushing, pushing me down to where no one day is a day free from fear, me--not even sure of who I am or what I fear.

But I do call. And Terrance asks me if I'd be free to come into the office to meet with Bill Knight, the other lawyer who is partnering with him on "my case." Bill just had a few additional questions--thought it might be good to get us all together in one room, you know, get us all on the same page, Terrance says. Sure, I say, and we set a time for Monday, setting me up for another weekend of anxiety in anticipation of this Monday meeting where we all get on some page, presumably the same one. Only *they* didn't find the damn body. *They* are not a person of interest. I did. I am. Me--the person I no longer know.

10

It's Saturday night and I find myself, most surprisingly, having dinner with Tad and Mariah. I am usually home on Saturday nights, date night, because, as my friends and I like to say, Saturday night is for amateurs. Meaning, Saturday nights draw crowds at restaurants and movies and "events," and crowds mean waiting and we hate to wait. And we don't really need to encounter the Saturday night mob scenes and lines and "wait," since we have six other nights of the week free and six mornings other than Sunday, because we're retired, in which to sleep in if we have had a late night, so why deal with the Saturday night frenzies? So, we don't.

Thus, it is doubly surprising that I'm out at all on a Saturday night, let alone out with Tad and Maria Worthington. Why. Well, Tad texted me in the morning saying he and Mariah were in town on "house business" and would be catching an early dinner before returning home (to some place in north Jersey, I still knew not where exactly)--so would I like to meet them at Alphonse, a local Italian restaurant, and share a meal? I thought it both peculiar and yet rather kind of Tad to extend this invitation, so I accepted perhaps too hastily, and we agreed to meet at six.

During the day, I had second and third thoughts, but reasoned that the event itself was probably harmless, it was a diversion, and I did like the food at Alphonse. In a few of his earlier texts, Tad had casually mentioned that we get together for dinner, so this invite was not totally out of the blue. I just hoped Tad had thought to make reservations otherwise the wait would be hopeless. Happily, he had, and when I arrive at six, the Worthingtons are waiting for me at the reception and we are shown immediately to a table, a nice one, in a cozy corner near the fireplace. The temperature has remained above freezing, but the night is still chilly and damp, so the fire is a welcome touch. We order cocktails and while we wait for them to come, Tad tells me that he has made arrangements for the tree removal during the first or second week of March, and that I needn't be home, but he will text me the precise date, in advance, once the tree people notify him.

Tad is looking his usual preppy self in grey slacks, dark blue blazer, blue shirt and rep tie, all very clean and starched, which is apparently his way. Mariah is as glamorous as ever, but understated in a calf-length black dress with a little bolero sweater of deep fuchsia on top, and black leather boots on bottom. Her gold Chanel chains glitter in the firelight and her hair, pulled back in an unadorned pony tail, creates an almost unnerving frame for the prominent cheekbones and sooty eyes that are the hallmark of that face. We talk a bit more about the tree removal and some previous experiences I've had with the process, and then the drinks are served, the evening's specials are described, and we turn our attention to our menus. I am pretty sure what I will have, having eaten here enough times to have developed some favorites, but Tad and Mariah are studying the menu with the care and time of relative newcomers. I ask if they've eaten here before and they both look rather surprised by the question and then say, no, in fact they haven't. They had just heard it was good. I tell them it is and that they can't go wrong--on either the specials or the regular menu. Just pick what you like and you won't be disappointed.

When the waiter returns for out orders, I am surprised that Mariah orders spaghetti and meatballs and Tad orders lasagna. These choices seem rather mundane to me, mundane for sophisticated diners which I assume the Worthingtons to be, but I just order my angel hair Boscomare, a wonderful blend of shellfish in a light, airy plum tomato and basil sauce, and make no comment on their selections.

They are easy talkers, the Worthingtons, and we find no scarcity of subjects. The talk turns for a short while to politics and Mariah asks me if I have read a certain book, one whose title I am unfamiliar with. She explains that it is a book about the corrupt activities of the "deep state" and that it is both eye-opening and shocking. Oh, wow, I say, trying to stay politically neutral, and ask like what's shocking, for instance. She tells me that according to the book's author, the entire FBI is a subversive organization that runs our government for power and profit. At a loss for a response, as this political view is foreign to me, I just say wow again--and I normally hate people who say wow. And then I ask, all 125,000 of the agents and special agents and secretaries and lawyers, like all of them? She nods quietly until Tad adds, well, it may be a bit exaggerated, but the guy who wrote it knows his stuff and has lots of evidence to back his theories. Interesting, I say. And am saved from having to make further comment, as our dinners arrive and change our focus. When the talk resumes, it is about the food, the service, the ambience of our surroundings, and no further conversation about the deep state or the FBI commences.

We do talk about progress on their house, some inevitable delays, local contractors. Tad sounds reasonably knowledgeable about the building process and I ask casually if he is employed in construction, but he just laughs and says I wish, and enlightens me no further. I don't push it. He then asks if I have had further contact with the police about "that matter" and I say no. None. I can be closed-mouthed, too, especially about "that matter." And what I said was true, a non-starter. I don't mention having turned "that matter" over to my lawyer. Less said the better. And then we go on talking until the meal comes to a pleasant end.

Driving home, I think about how truly mysterious the Worthingtons are. And what was all that deep-state conspiracy nonsense all about? I let myself wonder of they are in any way connected to the "matter," the murder, and I don't rule it out. I rule nothing out. I can understand their interest--prurient or self-referenced. But thoughts of their guilt peter out as there seems to be no visible connection at all between this glamorous couple and the son of my former grade-school classmate. Forget it, I think. Forget it all--until, of course, Monday.

I keep myself very busy on Sunday. After church and my weekly luncheon with the two couples I have dined with after church for years, I go to a local mall by myself and wander through Williams Sonoma and Ann Taylor with no intention of buying anything, but eventually do purchase a pretty silk scarf from Ann Taylor after all. I then stop in a kind of upscale take-out food place and get a chicken Kiev dinner "to go" to solve the endless question of what's for dinner. Still restless, I drive to the beach, parking in a lookout spot to just sit in my car, with many other Sunday sitters, watching the inlet, the ocean, the gulls, and a few fishermen who lean over the rail, their lines cast into the inlet. I wonder vaguely what they catch, if they eat it, if it's dinner or just sport. It's after three, so I decide to get on home and watch whatever golf tournament might be on. I miss football enormously in this fallow time after "the big game", the Super Bowl. And while I play golf and enjoy watching the tournaments on TV, nothing really works for me like football.

When I get home, I see I have a phone message from Jared. He's not a regular caller and most often only calls when there is a definite subject to discuss--business or family matters. But his message is casual, just checking in, call when you get a minute. So, after I feed the cats and put away my coat, my purse, my new scarf and my chicken dinner, I call him back. I get his answering machine--playing phone tag--so just leave a cheery message, all good, how are they, I'll be home for the rest of the day and evening, call back if convenient. But he doesn't. His call was probably just a welfare check and my return message served the purpose. I don't worry. Because no matter my nice day and purchases, my calming look at the ocean, I have a great deal more to worry about, if I want to worry. I don't want to. But I do.

11

My meeting with Terrance and the new lawyer, Bill Knight, at their office on Monday turns out to be a bit of a non-event, not something worth the worry I gave it. The office is pleasant, comfortable, and we greet when I get there and then move to have our talk in one of several conference rooms down one of the halls off the large reception area. I am impressed by the casual luxury of everything--the carpeting, furniture, fixtures, all elegant without being showy or overdone. We settle around a conference table, coffee is served by an assistant, and we all relax and smile. It feels like this is sort of a getting-to-know-you visit for Bill. He is older than Terrance and more conventionally lawyerly. He looks to be maybe early sixties, with dark hair, grey at the temples, wearing a very conventional and somewhat outdated dark grey pinstripe suit. He is soft-spoken but has sharp, dark eyes that seem to deserve the description of "piercing." He seems to be thinking more than he is saying, and really he says very little. The main focus is on reviewing my narrative, as Terry persists in calling it, and on occasion, Bill asks a question or clarifies something and adjusts his own notes. They ask for a few details that seem extraneous to me, like my travel schedule to San Diego--flight numbers, departure and arrival times, other passengers I might have taken particular note of in the airports or on the planes, in addition to Mr. Mooks. I also update the "narrative" by telling them about the guy in the gym who may or may not have been a detective and also about the dinner with Tad and Mariah on Saturday night. Terrance dutifully records these items in his chronology, but neither he nor Bill ask me any questions about either event.

Our meeting ends. Bill returns to his office, shaking my hand gently and smiling, while Terry walks me back to reception. He mentions casually that they are doing the investigations we had discussed and that he will let me know if anything pertinent emerges. He adds that it might be useful to get some background on Tad and Mariah, too, as they seem to be popping up rather frequently of late and I nod my agreement. I am unable to give him a home address or even a town for them--if they have ever mentioned it, I have forgotten--but I show Terry the text messages from Tad that have his mobile number. Then he, too, gently shakes my hand and I take my leave, out into the bright and cold February day. For some reason I actually feel comforted by this visit to Bill and Terry, able to ignore the dire undercurrents it suggests, perhaps mesmerized by the office's ambiance and the feeling of warmth and well-being it imparts.

As I drive home, I hear my mobile phone beeping at me signaling an incoming message, but I ignore it. I'll check when I get home, I think. But when I get home, I get distracted by the daily mail that has arrived while I was gone and then by getting myself some lunch and, after, cleaning up the kitchen. I sit down with a cup of coffee, turn on the TV, get interested in a program about a home renovation on HGTV--and so it is after 3:00 PM when I remember my previously beeping mobile phone. When I retrieve it and check my messages, I find a somewhat ominous text message: Call Phyllis. Phyllis, or Phil as we call her, is my friend Martha's daughter, and while we are friendly, we do not regularly text or communicate, so the message alerts me and I call immediately. Mom's in the hospital, she tells me. She's been shot. Suddenly, I can't breathe. Shot? I manage to squeak out? Shot? I say again. I feel incoherent, my insides trembling. Phil briefly explains that while her mother was out working in the garden late in the morning, she got a sudden sharp pain in her shoulder and heard a loud bang almost simultaneously. She had been kneeling and was knocked to the ground, but only when she managed to get herself into the house did she realize she was bleeding and was able to call 911. Oh my God, I'm saying, oh no, oh my God. How is she? What hospital? And then I repeat, shot? Who would shoot Martha?

I drive to the hospital immediately, only ten minutes away, my foot shaking on the gas the whole way, and meet Phil in the ER waiting room. She is a pretty, tall and slender woman, very like her mother. She is pale, but calm, and tells me Martha has been stabilized, waiting to be admitted and then taken up to surgery. At the moment, the police are with her and have asked Phil to leave while they conduct a preliminary interview. I ask if Martha saw anything or anybody and Phil says no, nothing to her knowledge. We hug each other and then sit back down to wait. Phil's husband Billy is on his way home from his office in New

York, but she has yet to call her children who are both away at school. Wait and see what happens, she says. Looks like Mom will be OK. The surgery is exploratory and to repair whatever they find, but right now she doesn't appear to be in immediate danger. Strong. She's strong, I say.

We sit in silence for a few minutes until a uniformed officer and two plainclothes men come through the door from the emergency facility. They confer for a minute or two and then one of the plainclothesmen heads towards us while the other two move to the exit. I am more than a little startled to see that this might be one of the men who interviewed me the day I discovered the body and, worse, the man I thought I saw, maybe following me, in the gym last week. I could feel my head go sort of light, dizzy. It is the first time that I consciously make a connection between the shooting of Willie Arthur and the shooting of my friend Martha. Could they be connected? *Of course* they could be connected, you idiot, my mind flashes out. Two shootings in one small town that had not had a shooting since--ever? Connected? Rocket science anyone? I process this in the few seconds it takes for the detective to approach us and, as he stands before us, "don't talk to the police" keeps echoing around my brain--Jared's mantra, Terry's mantra--but how could I not? The man is standing in front of us--greeting Phil and then me. I give a non-committal nod and then make the iron-clad assumption that he's come to talk to Phil--why not?--and that I will have no part in the conversation. After he tells Phil that her mom is doing very well, I smile, excuse myself tactfully, and then get up and move away, attempting to define my neutrality and appear polite, butting out of a conversation in which I don't belong, leaving the space to Phil and Mr. Cop. He seems uninterested in me, and I purposely move far enough away so that I can't hear what he's saying. Don't want to. I signal to Phil that I'm going back to see Martha and walk back to the desk to check and make sure that's all right. The desk clerk checks something on her computer, gives me a cubicle number, and nods in the affirmative that I can go visit--and I do, quickly and without looking back.

I find Martha's cubicle and am relieved to see that she looks good, normal, maybe a little pale but alert and smiling at a nurse who has stopped in to check her vitals. Martha leans back on her pillow with an IV in her arm and some EKG pasties on her upper chest and arm. Her right shoulder is heavily bandaged. She is wearing a hospital wrap on top, still has her jeans on below. She still has some vestiges of lipstick on her mouth and her hair is as neat as ever. Oh my dear Martha, I say, whatever is all this? She gives me a crooked smile and says, a little weakly, that she feels OK, shoulder hurts, although they've given her pain medication, so it's not too bad, and that she doesn't have a clue about any of this One minute I'm gardening, the next I'm flat on my face among the pachysandra. So, I say, never you mind; they'll just do a little patching up in surgery and in a few days you'll be right again. I hope, she says. I tell her Phil is talking to the police guy and will be back in a few, and then I just hold her hand and say no more. I'm thinking her talk with the cops probably exhausted her and she needs no more grilling from me. So we sit like this for a while until Phil returns, this time with Billy, her husband, who has gotten home and met up with her in the waiting room. Billy is a big strapping man, bald but still handsome, fit, and surprisingly gentle for such a large man. His tie is a little askew and he looks as if he's just driven from the city at the speed of light, but he is calm and soothing with Martha, holding Phil's hand reassuringly.

Eventually, they come to take Martha away to prep her for surgery. We are told that they really don't have a time frame for what they call "the procedure," but that after surgery, she will be taken to recovery and probably kept there for as long as eight hours and that only family can visit her in recovery and only for ten minutes every hour at best. Following that, she will go to her room, and will then be available during regular visiting hours. All of which is to say: Go home. To me. I squeeze Martha's hand and tell her I'll see her tomorrow morning. Phil tells me she'll text me whenever she knows anything and reluctantly, I watch my friend being wheeled out--and then I leave. Dear God watch over her and keep her safe.

Driving home from the hospital through the now-dark and frigid night, I let my thoughts wend back to the possible, very possible connection between the shooting of my "body" and the shooting of my friend. Could it be possible that the shooter, possibly the same shooter, somehow confused Martha with me? We had, after all, gone to the police station together that day after my discovery. And my name had never been mentioned nor my exact address given in any of the news accounts. Martha also, like me, lived slightly outside of town and somewhat close to the river, so it might be possible for that confusion to arise, although Martha had no outbuildings on her property and I was certain that my potting shed had been mentioned in all the news articles, several times, if not my address. But if someone had confused us, even though that seemed unlikely, could the bullet that slammed into her shoulder have been meant for me? Why? I had, after all, gotten a bullet in a box in my suitcase, inexplicable and now tucked away in Terry's file someplace. Guns, bullets, madness. I was suddenly very cold. I turned up the heat in the car, slowed down, and took stock. There were no cars behind me, a few ahead. No one turned when I turned off the highway to my road, but I drove slowly, passing my house and going once again around my curving street, my car a lone car in the night, and finally drove into my garage, waiting until the automatic garage door closed before exiting the car. I locked the door between the house and the garage immediately after entering and secured the blinds and drapes before turning on a few lights and re-setting my alarm system. Only then did I feel safe enough to breathe.

Until I remembered that person in my back garden a month ago in early January, that ill-defined shape outlined against the snow, crouching in the dark.

12

They say everything seems better in the morning, and everything did. A text from Phil assured me that Martha was doing very well, had been moved from recovery to her room, and was sleeping. The surgery had been fairly "routine," was all she said about that, said she'd fill me in later. Regular visiting hours were in effect, and I could see Martha from 2:00 to 4:00 PM, or from 7:00 to 9:00 PM. I knew I'd be there at 2:00 PM sharp.

It was a cold but brilliantly sunny morning, the winter shadows black against the sunny places, everything out there like an etching that could have been called "Cold." I checked the thermometer on my deck and it registered 14 degrees. This was headed toward being the coldest February since 1997, according to the local weather forecaster. There was no mention on the news, as yet, of Martha's shooting, but I guessed that it would only be a matter of time before it became "breaking news" on one or more of the newscasts. Cable, probably.

I felt as if I should call Terrance to advise him of Martha's shooting, but that somehow would seem as if I had made the connection between Martha and Willie Arthur and I was as yet unwilling or unable to do that positively. I kept hoping that it was some kind of misguided hunter or the accident of a local gun owner rather than a serial shooter, one who was perhaps gunning for me. So I worked on distracting myself by making an elaborate breakfast--pancakes, bacon, home fries, yogurt and fruit--a breakfast so huge that I could barely look at it once I'd plated it. But I persisted, eating slowly, around the edges, munching on the bacon, flooding the pancakes with far too much syrup, over-salting the potatoes. I finally gave up and scraped the remains into the garbage.

Later in the morning, the telephone rang. As had become my habit, I let it go to message--I could always call whomever it was back later, say I had been in the shower. But it turned out it was Phil, so I quickly picked up as she started to leave a message, fearful that maybe she was about to tell me that Martha had taken a turn for the worse. But, no, Phil was just calling to repeat what she had texted earlier, just to be sure I had gotten the message. She told me a bit more about the surgery, that it had been a pretty clean shoot, damaged tissue, fractured clavicle, but all repairable, repaired, and promised to heal well without any lasting impacts except probably a stiff shoulder for a few months. It will be about four to six weeks before she heals and begins therapy, Phil added, for her to be "good as new," as the surgeon told her. I felt enormously relieved, thanked Phil for the call, told her I'd see her that afternoon at the hospital.

Just as I hung up and turned away from the phone, it rang again and I answered it quickly, reflexively, without thoughts of Terrance or the police, or anyone else.

It is Jared, my son. And he is frantic. Apparently news

of Martha's shooting made the news app that he uses to stay in touch with home news. The report gave all the gory details, including Martha's full name and address and the circumstances of the shooting. I'm coming to stay with you, Jared is saying. This is serious, dangerous, and you cannot be alone. If the g-d police won't give you protection, he is saying, then I will. I try to dissuade him, try my weak logic that the two shootings may not be related, that we should at least wait until we find out a bit more about Martha's shooting which may, for all we know, be some kind of freaky accident and have nothing to do with the murder in the shed. No, Jared says, absolutely not. I'm coming. I have a flight later this morning, will rent a car at the airport, and should be with you about ten PM. Well, I say weakly, that sounds pretty definite. And to tell the truth, I find myself sort of exhaling, maybe relaxing, giving in and then feeling some kind of enormous relief. But, I'm a mother, so I say: What about your work? How can you just leave? He tells me he can manage, can do a lot on his computer, shift some work to his partner whom he has already contacted. It's done, Mom, he says. See you tonight. We'll talk and make some sensible arrangements. I'm not sure what he means by this, but before I can ask, he is gone.

He has hung up and I am standing there, happy, relieved, but also with a dawning awareness that there *is* a reason Jared is coming--and that reason is terrifying.

I clean up the rest of the breakfast detritus, repress all fearful thoughts for the time being, shower, dress, and head to the supermarket, suddenly aware that if Jared is coming, and he is, I will have to stock up. Normally, I shop for one. But today in the store, I roam the aisles and load up on meals, snacks, drinks--anything I think of that he might want, like, need. I was sort of like a crazy lady but only when I checked out and saw that I had spent almost two hundred dollars did it occur to me that I had been mildly hysterical, had bought enough food for ten people. So what, I think. It'll keep. I wheel the bags out to my car and as I open the trunk, nearly jump out of my skin when a voice very close asks if I want some help. I peer around the trunk hood and see a pleasant-looking man, one I had never seen before, smiling and tentatively holding out a hand. But instead of appreciating what was probably the kindness of a stranger, I freeze in fear and just keep saying no, no, I'm OK, so no. And then I say no again, very loud. The man bows his head, looks confused, but moves away as I rapidly stuff the shopping bags into my trunk.

I pull out of my parking space too quickly, narrowly avoid hitting a car waiting for my space, and drive way too fast out of the parking lot and onto the avenue. I catch myself. Calm down, for God's sake. Calm. I slow down my speed and say like a mantra: Jared is coming. Jared is coming. I drive the familiar streets working on a safe speed and then start to consider the man in the supermarket parking lot. Had I ever seen him before? I truly didn't think so. Could he have been a cop? He really didn't look that spiffy--was kind of gangly and maybe too old? He'd had white hair that was kind of longish, and wore glasses. He had on an overcoat and scarf. Oh my God. Was this what it was coming to? Even a kind stranger becoming a threat? I shook my head to shake away the suspicions and drove on home, safely and sensibly.

By the time I had the groceries put away and had coffee

and toast for lunch--not hungry after my misguided huge breakfast--it is time to leave for the hospital.

Again, I drive slowly, carefully, aware of my surroundings, relatively cheery at the prospect of seeing Martha and even happier at the thought of Jared's visit. Because we live so far apart, I never think of my son as a part of my life. He is my son and I love him, but we live two different lives on two very different coasts. Somewhere, though, I always know in my heart that he is there for me, a reliable man who will understand his mother's needs and never abnegate his responsibilities. Somehow, however, I never thought of these responsibilities as having to do with murder and shooting and the thought that his mother was either a target--or a suspect--or both. How incredible, really.

I get to the hospital a little after two, chat briefly with the lady at the visitors' desk, get my pass, and make my way to Martha's room. Hospitals are labyrinthine, illogical halls and pass ways, always confusing and disconcerting. One wanders the byways, gets on and off what one hopes is the right elevator, and is suddenly in the midst of something terribly private and disheveled. There are people glimpsed in rooms, sprawled on their beds in pajamas, hospital issue, that are institutional and washed out, pajamas gaping at unexpected places. There are food carts in hallways, IV bags draped over metal carriers, half-eaten meals on tray tables. People are sleeping or lying back with mouths half open while someone sweeps their room. Caregivers bustle about, visitors wander in and out of rooms. Some patients walk the halls slowly. It is the oddest combination of activity and stasis, order and disorder. It is a limbo, where real life is a memory and a hope. It makes me shiver.

But I find Martha's room, at the end of a short hall, without trouble. I am disturbed at first by the police officer stationed outside her door and a bit agitated when he asks for my identification and checks it against a computer printout he consults, but then I begin to find this "precaution" reassuring. The woman has, after all, just been shot. The lack of a police presence would be more disturbing.

She has a private room, with just her bed, and then a chintz covered couch and easy chair against the wall opposite with a pretty lamp on a table next to the chair. She has a big window, currently partially shaded, with a park-like view. Her patient space and general environment seem markedly orderly and calm, which pleases me. She is sitting up in bed, her right shoulder heavily bandaged and braced and she is sipping from a plastic cup that she holds a bit awkwardly in her left hand. She looks sleepy, but well. Her color has returned, the strained look modified. I smile. She smiles.

I take off my coat and ask Martha if she's ok, if she needs anything, can I do anything before settling myself into the arm chair as Martha insists that all is well, that she needs nothing, and for God's sake, sit. I still can't believe this, I say and Martha says she too has a strange feeling of displacement, that somehow she should still be back in the garden doing winter chores, removing old tomato stakes, pulling out dead Mums, collecting old pots missed in the fall clean up--anything but lying in a hospital bed. But, she goes on, everyone has been wonderful. The surgeon knows his stuff, is very informing, very positive and the staff has been attentive and caring, gentle. The pain is much, much better. And no one, she says emphatically, says *anything* about how

I got here--you know, the shooting thing. I wonder if this is a hint to me to zip it about the shooting, no questions, no agonizing over the mystery. But then as I smile and say nothing, she goes on. The detective was back here earlier to ask me if I remembered anything else, anything at all odd, different, especially in the last few days. I told him no, nothing, she goes on, until it dawned on me that there was something that was nagging at my mind, something about a car. It's not the proverbial strange car in the neighborhood thing, Martha says vaguely, but something else, just can't put my finger on it, memory won't come. Well, I said, it will, eventually, you know. The less you worry it, the faster you'll remember. Yes, she said, I think so. I told the detective that.

I want to ask her if it was Detective Eggers, hoping not, still hoping there is no connection between Martha's case and the Willie Arthur case, but before I can ask, Martha identifies him as Detective Lu, a young Asian man, very soft spoken and courteous. I smile hoping my relief and the reasons thereof are not too obvious. But just at that moment, we are both distracted by Phil's arrival. She comes in with a shopping bag full of things and a big bouquet of flowers. She pulls a vase from the bag into which she deposits the flowers, and then takes out a robe and slippers for Martha, some books and magazines--and for several minutes, Phil and I are busy unpacking the bag, getting water for the flowers, draping Martha's robe around her shoulders, arranging the books and magazines on her bedside table, and trying to figure a way we can brew the herb tea that Phil has also brought. I offer to check at the nurse's station and by the time I return with a carafe of boiling water and three cups, I find Martha and Phil discussing medical details, all thoughts of detectives gone. Just as well.

The next hour is spent sipping tea, eventually speaking of subjects much lighter than a shooting and complicated medical issues, and the name Willie Arthur never comes up, thankfully. It is clear to me after our tea party that it's time for me to go and let Phil get Martha comfortable and ready for a nap. I kiss Martha gently on the forehead, a forehead cool and smooth, and feeling very reassured that my friend will be well and that she is in a good place, I say my good-byes and leave.

By five o'clock, I am hungry and so put a piece of salmon into the oven to bake and then make some creamed spinach while my fish cooks. I pour myself a generous glass of white wine and put another bottle in the fridge in case Jared will want some when he gets here. I tune into a local cable channel but either I have missed it or there was just no report on Martha's shooting. The weather report is gloomy, freezing temps, chance of snow, up to two inches overnight. Winter, winter. I switch to the golf channel and idly watch men play their game somewhere that the sun is shining. I eat, wash up, and then pick up my book, planning to read until Jared gets here.

The phone rings and I let it go to message. It's Terrance, my lawyer, and so I pick up. I'm not anxious to talk with him, but feel obligated. He is slightly abrupt and dispenses with pleasantries to tell me that the ballistic report is in and that, yes, the bullet taken out of Martha was fired from the same gun as the one that killed Willie Arthur. Connection. He said Detective Eggers called to tell him and that as a result, he and Detective Lu were now combining their investigation, with Eggers taking the lead. He has asked Terry to find out if I have "any thoughts" on this connection and I tell Terry my theory, that someone who is after *me* had accidentally confused Martha and me and shot her by mistake, maybe someone who thinks I know more about the Arthur killing than I actually do. I tell Terry he can share these "thoughts" with Eggers if he thinks that advisable. I also tell him that Jared is coming tonight and Terry says good, good. We should meet, the three of us, soon. Terry also says he has some feedback from the various investigations he's running, but will wait to tell me until we meet. As much as I'd like to know what he's discovered, I say OK, OK. Let's wait--and arrange for him to come to my house and meet with Jared and me tomorrow afternoon. More agita. Always more agita.

When Jared finally arrives at almost ten-thirty, we hug a bit longer and stronger than is usual for us and I find that I am enormously happy and relieved to see him, much more relieved than I had expected to be. I look at him, my son, with his perennial light tan, his even features so like his father's, his solid build, a bit over six feet, his crisp dark hair cut short, and his lovely deep blue eyes. He got my eyes, I think vaguely. He is so handsome and strong--just so *there.* His presence makes my life feel more normal than it has felt in a long time.

I bring him up to date on everything--Martha, Terry's call--while we share a glass of wine and some cheese and crackers. By midnight, we are both tired beyond any more talk, kiss goodnight, and retire. I sleep very soundly knowing somewhere in my head that Jared is in the guest room just down the hall and that I can finally, finally relax.

13

Jared and I both sleep late and I am awakened finally by two hungry cats, gently pawing at my face. I am surprised to see it is after eight already. It is, of course, only 5 AM west coast time, so I will let Jared sleep on for a while. I put on a pot of coffee, feed the cats, then take a quick shower and dress casually, but decently enough that I won't have to change for Terrance's visit later. Sweater, slacks, same old me. My new scarf and gold earrings help. When I am back in the breakfast room drinking coffee, Jared emerges from his room, fills a mug, and joins me at the table. He is still in his pajamas and robe, eyes a bit blurry. Like me, Jared is a quiet morning person, not big on chatter in the AM. He looks sleepy, but I think rested. We glance at the TV, filled with political news, the norm lately, and sit quietly. Eventually, Jared stretches and asks if I'd like to go somewhere for brunch and that sounds delightful to me, so I say yes, suggest a local place he knows that serves a lovely brunch, in a small hotel in town on the river, and Jared goes off to shower and dress.

By 10:30 AM we are seated at a pleasant table in the hotel dining room, a small and cozy room with windows on three sides, overlooking the river and the landscape over which a light blanket of snow has fallen overnight, each of us enjoying a Bloody Mary as we wait for our food. There will be a grapefruit half, and then pancakes and sausage for me, French toast and bacon for Jared. The room has only a handful of people, not unusual for mid-week during the winter, but it's nice, quiet voices and pleasant smells emanating from the kitchen. I always liked this place, Jared is saying, even though quaint isn't usually my style. I know, I agree, same with me.

Jared brings up the subject of my safety again, reviewing the options he briefly mentioned last night. He can only stay with me for a limited number of days after all and so wants something more permanent done for my safety. His favorite idea is for me to come back to San Diego with him and stay there for the duration until these crimes are solved. I don't reject that idea out of hand, but it is not my first choice. I have Harry, Martha, my friends, my home--and the kitties--all of which I'd have to leave behind for God knows how long: So many arrangements, too much that I'd miss. And regardless of how well meaning and loving Jared and Lucy are--still, having anyone else, even me, living in their house would be an intrusion, no matter how they think they'd feel. The holiday visit is fun and busy, but in the end, if I went back now, I'd have little to do, would rely solely on Lucy all day to amuse me--I can only read and knit for so long-- and, well, I'd hate that kind of imposition. I don't say any of this yet, waiting to review the other options. Jared mentions having cameras installed in various spots around the house and the property, hiring a security agency, even hiring a personal body guard or guards. He wants a regular police patrol and suggests that perhaps I should consider getting a guard dog. He mentions the possibility of me moving in temporarily with a friend here or perhaps even renting another place to live close by, not telling anyone where. I delay having to respond to any of this by suggesting that we talk all of it over with Terrance this afternoon. He may have some other thoughts, I say. And then our food arrives and Jared agrees that getting Terry's input would be good. And so we eat--and talk about other things. Nice other things.

Terrance arrives promptly at 3:00 PM, and we adjourn as usual to the breakfast room with coffee and, this time, some small stylish cupcakes Jared and I have picked up at the bakery after we finished brunch. Terrance nibbles on a cupcake as Jared starts talking about "my security," his prime issue, he emphasizes to Terrance. Terrance agrees that we must discuss this but first, he says, between bites, let me update you on some information. To begin with, he starts, wiping some gooey icing off his fingers with the little tea napkins I've set out, the police investigation is getting complicated, according to my sources. Of course, no one is allowed to discuss an ongoing investigation so we don't really know anything for sure--some gossip and slips of the tongue, nothing we can really pin down. But, there is a pretty solid rumor that the feds are somehow involved in the case--not sure which feds or why, but definitely involved. This seems to us to suggest that some federal criminal activity might be related to the shootings--maybe organized crime, drugs, gun smuggling, human trafficking--no way to know. But this seems to point even further away from your mom being involved. Worth a small sigh of relief, we believe. Jared asks a few questions, but I know he is thinking what I am thinking: Timmy Mooks, a spook, a fed spook, as Jared once surmised. We don't mention this, but Terrance seems to intuit our thoughts, because he goes on to say that their investigations of "the players," as he calls them, have turned up quite a bit, but precious little information on Mr. Mooks. Jared raises an eyebrow, but says nothing and lets Terrance continue.

As for Morty Arthur, your former little elementary school classmate, he continues, he died three years ago. He seems to have lived a relatively blameless life--married, two children, Willie the oldest and a younger daughter, worked in various sales positions all his life, lived in Manhattan until he retired, moved to Florida, died there six years later, surviving widow still living there. His daughter is married and living in Colorado. It gets slightly more interesting with his son, Willie, deceased and found in your shed. He was apparently something of a black sheep in the family, several minor criminal arrests, convictions, probations, a six-month stint for petty theft until he hit the jackpot, fifteen years for armed robbery, of which he served twelve years in Attica. This, of course, not only puts him in bad company but also strongly suggests possession of a weapon or weapons. His whereabouts were unknown after he completed his three year probation five years ago--until, of course, he turned up dead in your shed. So, I say softly, a little crook, our Willie. Or, Terrance adds, a little crook getting bigger.

As for the Worthingtons, your soon-to-be-neighbors, mixed results. Both graduated from Penn State, probably met there. She worked as a fashion photographer's model in New York for a few years after graduation until she married Tad, ten years ago, in a kind of society-type wedding, her father a minor New York millionaire with pretensions. Tad was at the time employed in a training program with Morgan Chase, but left soon after his marriage to Mariah to become self-employed as a financial consultant. After that, the information gets a bit more difficult to pin down. They are the registered owners of a town house in Bergen County, NJ, but limited surveillance and some talks with neighbors seem to suggest that they are "hardly ever" there. They also own a partnership in a house in the Hamptons, apparently a rental-income property registered to a limited partnership that has been very hard to trace. Personal information, financials, leisure activities have all been equally as difficult to pin down, aside from a few society-page mentions of their having been present at some event or other--a tennis tournament party, charity fund raiser, cocktail gala-- not much about who they are or why they're at these events. So we are considering them a mystery couple at the moment. Nothing suspicious as much as just nothing at all. Some people guard their privacy for very legitimate reasons, so we are really nowhere with them.

Terrance checks his notes and seemingly satisfied that he's exhausted that report, looks at us and says: So, the problem seems to be, who are we guarding your mother against? The only one on the list that seems truly and recognizably dangerous is Willie Arthur--and he's dead. So who is roaming your town, shooting people--and why? Who is sneaking a bullet into your luggage and why? Who is calling you, hanging up, and sneaking around your garden in the snow--and, again, why? He lifts his hands, palms up, and just looks at us--and we look back. Who and why, indeed.

The options are really numerous, Terrance continues, but we think, other than the default legendary "psychopath stalking the town," rarely the actual killer in reality, we believe that the idea that the killer is some friend, foe, or associate of Willie Arthur's makes the most sense. Hypothetically, he (or she) shot Willie, and then shot Martha. We don't think shooting Martha was a mistake--mistakenly thinking she was you, that is--because, after all, the shooter most likely had to know where he left the body and so would know who you are and where you live. We think shooting Martha was some kind of warning to you, or possibly a second (attempted) murder in an effort to confuse and throw off police about the first. It's almost impossible to know anything, but right now, those are our best guesses, which, as Jared has said, makes your security now paramount, as far as we're concerned. I've shared these thoughts with Eggers, and he has agreed to provide regular police patrols of your house. But we don't believe that's enough. Since Eggers was very unhappy about the thought of you leaving for San Diego, and we are inclined to think that flight is often an indicator of guilt, we are not sure that's the best choice. At the moment, you can't be stopped from doing that, but it's reasonable to assume that travel there could easily be traced--which then brings up the issue of putting Jared and his family in danger, too.

I raise my hand to stop Terrance. I say that I am not going to put Jared and Lucy and the boys in danger under any circumstances and that while I dislike the idea of making my home a little fortress, I'm inclined to think that adding security measures, whatever kind he thinks would be useful, and relying on Eggers' promise for police patrols would be a good way to begin. I can be very careful about going out alone, I add, and think that visible signs of home security might provide a needed deterrent. Jared is looking uncomfortable during my little speech and starts to say something--but Terrance interrupts to say that he has called a very reliable local security agency and has written out a protection plan, one that they can provide and that he approves, and that installation can start tomorrow, with Jared around to supervise.

Jared shrugs, lifts an eyebrow, and jokes about being outnumbered, but seems inclined to agree. I can stay until at least the end of the week, he says, and supervise Mom's use of the system, feel it out, see if it is practicable. But, if I have any doubts, any at all, then she's coming home with me. OK? Terrance and I look at each other and then at Jared, and then nod--silently, maybe a bit skeptically, but as he has agreed to our terms, we agree to his.

The next day is incredibly chaotic with men swarming all over my house and property, installing spy TV cameras, alarms, motion lights, and God knows all what in and out, up and down. A switch panel is installed in my pantry with a myriad of buttons and lights and I feel I will need to take a course in security management to handle it all, but the head installer says, no, because all will be monitored "24-7" from their offices and my little panel of buttons and light is mainly to inform me of any irregularities, irregularities that will trigger calls to the police and to their offices. He is a very reassuring man, tall, lanky, low key and seems to feel that "we have this all buttoned up," as he puts it, "tight, very tight." Most importantly, Jared seems largely impressed, especially about the off-site monitoring and the promise of a 5-minute response team and the police alert system. After all the installations are done, numerous tests are run and we're finally informed, just as we finish dinner, that "all systems are go." One closet is in the process of being fitted out as a "panic space," new steel doors to be installed with sturdy interior locks, vented to outside air, stocked with water bottles and health bars--and with the somewhat grim instructions that if I feel at any time that an intruder has gained entrance, to head for the panic closet, lock myself in with the automatic push-button lock, and press the panic button. The entire explanation and view of the construction of this facility makes me deeply claustrophobic, but Jared seems very comfortable with this "final solution." The installer tells us he will return in a few days to finish the installation of the panic space but that all else is currently operational, and with that, he leaves while Jared and I just look at each other and say, almost in unison, My God.

14

The remainder of Jared's stay is pleasant, uneventful and by the time he leaves today, Sunday, he is comfortable--and I am comfortable--that I have the hang of the system and the security control panel. The panic space has been completed and outfitted, and if you didn't know what it is, you wouldn't know what it is. It looks from the exterior exactly like the innocent walk-in closet it has always been. I've tested it, and although it feels claustrophobic to me, it also lends a sense of security, albeit in a fearful sort of way.

Martha is being released from the hospital tomorrow, on Monday, and is already scheduled for physical therapy to begin, as soon as her healing has sufficiently progressed. Her family has also been busy having a security system installed for her, but Martha will spend her first month out of the hospital at Phil's house, recuperating there. Jared and I have visited her--short visits--a few times and she and I speak on the phone daily, and the one bright light in all this horror is that she sounds well, strong, and professes to be nearly pain free. Just aches sometimes, she says. Terrance has checked in by 'phone and is pleased with the outcome of the security installation. He has no further news, or at least none that he is sharing--and so all is stasis.

I can keep the security system on its "day setting" which enables me to open some doors, receive mail delivery, and exit in my car via the garage and driveway. From my car via mobile phone, I can set the system to the "night" setting and so completely secure the property while I'm out, if I'm out. All those groceries I bought for Jared's visit, however, have given me enough stock that I needn't shop for a while. And to be honest, I have no desire to go out, to encounter strangers who may be killers or policemen trailing me. I will be house-bound, I think, with some trepidation. I have forfeited going to church this morning, blamed it on my emotional fatigue after the last week, and have called Don and Kathy, my Sunday morning brunch companions, to cancel that, too. Kathy sounds very understanding and empathetic without saying specifically why, for which I am grateful.

It's very cold today and it has snowed lightly again last night, not enough accumulation to shovel, thank goodness, or to interfere with Jared's limo to the airport, but enough to make me shiver every so often, to turn up the heat and make more coffee. Harry and I had tentatively arranged to have dinner out tonight and I suddenly decide to go after all, to break my house-bound plan, in order to tell him at last the bare bones of the story that I have thus far withheld from him, withheld mostly to avoid talking about it and thereby giving my mind and my fears a hiatus. But I think now that someone I love and trust, someone other than Terrance and Martha, should know what's what, someone whom I know would be there for me if "something happened," although I don't specifically define for myself that "something."

So, while I hesitated when Harry called to confirm dinner tonight, feeling once again that now that I had built a fortress, I should shelter in place, I finally pushed that feeling down. I did not, after all, regardless of canceling this morning's church and brunch routine, want to be fully house bound, to be imprisoned in a home that I loved--but imprisoned nonetheless. Someone could shoot you in the restaurant, I think. Doubtful, but possible, no? Well, unlikely, I think. This person is a sneaky shooter, an ambusher--not a madman shooting people down in public. Killers have an MO, right? And this is not a crazed killer, but a calculating one who does not take inordinate risks. Even the daytime shooting of Martha was done in a remote locale with several secure exit routes. So, I talked myself into dining out with Harry. I can usually talk myself into anything, like everyone else, for good or for ill.

At six, Harry picks me up and we drive out of town, north, to a restaurant we both like and that I have chosen, probably for security reasons--since it is some distance from my home and not a place we frequent. As we drive away from my house, I take out my phone and punch in the "night" setting for my security system and Harry asks what I am doing, and that launches me into an explanation that takes the thirty minute drive to the restaurant to complete. Harry is quiet as I talk, interrupting only once or twice to ask a question or two for clarification. We arrive at the restaurant, get out of the car for the valet to park, go inside, leave our coats in the check room, and then get seated at a table we prefer, a table that Harry had requested when he made the reservation. The lights are low, the decor is art nouveau, the waiter who takes our drink orders is soft-spoken, and I find myself letting out a long breath, waiting to hear what Harry will say now that he is equipped with all the details of my sordid narrative. He smiles and we sit in silence casually looking at the menu, waiting for the drinks to arrive. When they do, we take a sip and then Harry asks, very quietly, if I feel secure in my home. As I think about my feelings of security, he goes on, quietly and somewhat reservedly, to say, because you could stay with me, you know. I keep thinking about whether or not I *do* feel secure in my home, even with all that additional technological paraphernalia surrounding me, and also what it would be like to "stay" with Harry.

He lives in a penthouse condo in a large complex that overlooks the ocean. Several years after his wife's death, he eventually sold the family home and decided he could, after all, put up with the impersonality of condo living in exchange for the convenience. The complex offers a weekly house cleaning service, a laundry service, on-request meal deliveries, security--all things that help Harry live his single life in reasonable comfort, even though he still misses his garden and his privacy. The staff at the condo complex are helpful and discreet, but they are always there. Watching. He does have an outdoor terrace with ocean views, and he keeps a thriving little garden out there--in pots and planters. He has a live ficus tree in his living room. I smile as I think of his altered but, in many ways, lovely, even luxurious, way of life. Could I share it? Even temporarily?

I say to him that I'm not sure--about either, but I am so grateful to him for his offer and do not rule it out. We go on to speak of other options, both of us agreeing that a retreat to San Diego is probably premature. In some ways, he says, I think if someone wanted to harm you--and forgive me if this is blunt--but they have had ample opportunity to do so already. What has changed that would make you a target *now*? I mean, he says, whomever it was that killed this guy and shot at Martha knows you don't know anything. If you did, he'd be in jail by now. What would be his motive to harm you? In fact, keeping you alive and a "person of interest" is to his benefit, no? It's true, I say. It's occurred to me as well that I am a kind of insurance policy for him. As long as the police waste their time on me, they're not looking at--or for--him. Or, maybe they are, I say, always unsure what to conclude about what the police really are doing. I just seem like such an absurd "person of interest," I continue, and cannot think that the police could be so stupid as to think I could be the killer--or *a* killer. I mean, it's almost a joke--short little old lady killer joke, you know? Well, he smiles slowly, you're not short--and you're not old, as in infirm or dotty. And you don't have little white curly hair, either, he says. I smooth my hair, self-consciously, my blondish bob that I've more or less worn for years, and tell Harry that flattery is both accepted and appreciated. Young at heart, I say and laugh and take another sip of my drink, feeling good.

And then just as we finish our appetizers, the lights go out. They flicker a little and then go off entirely and the only remaining light in the restaurant comes from the little candles flickering on each table. The conversational murmurs become expressions of surprise and then disbelief and then loud questions. What the hell? What's going on? A few diners get up and move toward the reception table and then just as the discontent mounts to shouts, the lights flicker and return, somewhat dimly, and the hostess asks for quiet, for everyone to be seated. She explains that there has been a power outage in the area but that the restaurant's generator has kicked in and will keep power on. She further explains that this will cause some dinner delays, depending upon the order, but that the restaurant will gladly excuse anyone who wishes to leave, without charge. She says the servers will explain the food delays to each party and asks only that there not be a mass exodus, that the car valets be given the appropriate time to deliver the cars to patrons. She concludes that she has no information about the cause or duration of the outage, is very sorry, and wishes us all a pleasant evening.

Harry and I remain silent throughout this little drama and now agree to wait and see what the outage has done to our dinner order. As it turns out, Harry's will be delayed, but mine will not, so we decide to share my dinner, cancel Harry's, and then stay for coffee. We'd have to wait for our car anyway, we decide, so why not relax while we do it?

About an hour later, we depart, sorry about the disruption, but still quite happy with the outcome of the evening, not really ruined at all. As we exit and look around, we see that the area surrounding the restaurant is in almost complete darkness, no streetlights, no house or store lights, a few candles seen flickering through windows of nearby houses, the sound of a generator groaning somewhere close. As we drive away, Harry turns on the car radio to try to get news about the outage and we are surprised to hear that the outage is almost county-wide, with about 300,000 people out of power. The cause has something to do with the power grid, but the radio announcer seems confused on this point. I wonder idly at first as to whether my town, my house will be out. It's eerie driving down the darkened parkway with only the headlights of other cars providing illumination--and fewer cars than usual as everyone has been advised to stay home until power returns. Then suddenly I wonder about my home security system. If the power is out, will my system be operational? I ask Harry and he suggests I call to find out. What I find out is that yes, the power is out in our town, my house included, and that the security company cannot give any guarantees that the system is still fully a go. They are working on that. Further calls inform us that Harry's condo which is south of the outage area has full power. The implications seem obvious.

Harry is fairly adamant that I will spend the night at his condo, and when I mention the cats, he logically points out that they will be fine, will sleep, have dry food to snack on, and that we will probably have power in the morning, at which time I can return home and feed the cats. He goes on to say that whatever is or is not working in my system, he is fairly sure I will have lost the exterior motion lights, and that exterior cameras will have little to photograph in the dark. He convinces me finally, and so we pass my exit on the parkway and see, as we head south, that eventually we are surrounded by normal lighting.

I immediately start thinking about sleeping at Harry's, what necessities I don't have in the way of provisions for a sleep over, and, of course, what his neighbors will think. He laughs at this latter point--says they'll think he's a gentleman providing aid to a lady in distress--and points out that he has a two-bedroom, two bath apartment and is sure he can provide both a clean tee shirt for me to sleep in and a new toothbrush, soap, towels--what's the problem? No, there are none, I think, and am suddenly enormously grateful to have this delightful port in the storm in which to have shelter in the face of this completely absurd and unexpected reality.

Our arrival and access to Harry's condo is completely easy and comfortable. The valet takes the car and, so we don't appear to be sneaking in, as we wait for the elevator Harry tells the fellow at the front desk that he is having a guest for the night due to the power outage. The man smiles at me and probably thinks how cute these old folks are. We take the elevator up to the top and enter the large foyer that serves Harry's penthouse apartment and the one opposite, only these two apartments up here.

The foyer is beautifully appointed as is Harry's apartment. I have only been here a few times in the past, mostly for relatively large social gatherings--a cocktail party, a Super Bowl party--once for a dinner party of six, two or three times with Harry alone. So, I know the place but still am struck once again by how lovely the decor is. Everything is done in muted grey shades, with a lot of white and a few black accents. Harry first groused about how impersonal it seemed when he first saw what the decorators had done, but he has managed, over time, to add just enough personal touches to make the place seem lived in, comfortable and, if not exactly "homey," stylish and definitely his. He has an interesting art collection, eclectic, colorful, but reserved. He has a few statuaries and one impressive granite sculpture done by a friend of his which is startling, simple, ragged but geometrical, standing apart on its pedestal, spotlighted from above. It reminds me vaguely of a sailing ship, but when I once asked Harry, he said his friend told him it was entitled "Shape #10". I have called it ship Shape in my own mind ever since and I like it and smile upon seeing it again.

I leave my coat in the hall closet and then make my way into the living room to the long, comfy couch and gratefully sink into its downy cushions and generous assortment of throw pillows. Harry flicks on the gas fireplace and then asks if I'd like a brandy to which I reply yes, and yes. We smile.

Harry and I have a very uncomplicated sexual life. We no longer have one. We had our share of passion in the past, mutually satisfying and appropriate. But as we continued to age, with a natural decline in passion and some age-related physical limitations, we just slipped out of the sexual component of our relationship. We spoke of it briefly and without rancor, happy with the deep friendship we had remaining to us. And that was that. There was no blame, no impatient longings, no feeling we had "lost" anything. We apparently had, fortunately, aged along the same path and allowed that we were beyond the age of passion. Regrets? Of course! Who would not love to be once again young enough for sexual excitement and pleasure? But human dignity and physical prohibitions are realities, too. No needless fumbling, failed Viagra experiments, eventual embarrassments, disappointments, judgments, none of that. As Harry once said, simply, if you can't, you don't.

So we enjoyed our brandy, our conversation, and as we both began to yawn, we smiled and Harry provided me with the aforementioned new tee shirt and tooth brush. We embraced, and I headed to the guest bathroom while he retired to his master bedroom suite.

I slept amazingly well and dreamlessly and managed to get myself together in the morning without too much stress. Fortunately, I had enough make up in my purse to look a little less than frightful, and simply pulled my hair back into a pony tail with a scrunchy. It's not my best look, but it was the best I could manage and Harry seemed not even to notice as I joined him in the kitchen for juice, coffee and some fresh bagels he had delivered. It was a little before seven o'clock and the sun had just come up over the dull grey February ocean, visible through all of the windows on this side of the apartment, very bright and dramatic. We learned from the TV news that the power was back on in most parts of the county, still no clear explanation for the outage, but back on except for a few remaining districts in the north. We assumed that meant my power was back and so we left about eight to get me back home and back to the kitties, about whom I worried too much, which Harry viewed with amused tolerance.

As we drove into my driveway, everything looked fine. I didn't even bother looking at my home security app on my phone, figuring I'd check the control panel when I got in, and call the company, no matter. Harry insisted on coming in with me and it was then that we discovered the horror. My house had been broken into, my fortress breached, and destruction was left behind.

15

We entered my house through the garage and what greeted us was an incredible, tragic mess--in my office and in the breakfast room, the two rooms that were immediately visible. Harry's first instinct was to leave and call the police, unsure as to whether the intruders still remained in the house--wise thinking, but not enough to restrain me from racing through the breakfast room anyway, running into the kitchen, and through to the rest of the house, looking and calling for my cats. Oddly, what I saw was reassuring, if one can ever be reassured while still in shock. But my house, beyond the breakfast room, seemed reasonably in tact and the kitties came racing down the hall, meowing loudly, to greet me, apparently coming from under my bed, their default place of refuge.

Still in the breakfast room, Harry called the police while I cuddled and then fed the cats and then joined him and started to look around. The main point of attack was clearly the pantry closet in which the security panel had been installed. It had been pulled apart, bare wires protruding from the wall, and some substance seemed to have been sprayed all over that side of the closet, something shiny and sticky, glue-like. The farm table was scored as if someone had raked a sharp object over it and the chair pads had all been slashed. Dishes and glasses had been flung from the shelf of the pie chest and lay shattered on the floor. I felt tears welling up--and then a slow, vicious anger start to build. I turned back into my office where drawers stood open, papers and books were thrown all over the floor--and my computer was not on my desk, or anywhere that I could see. My love seat cushions had been slashed, the desk chair overturned, my Persian carpet sliced in several places. My tears and anger left me as I stood there, overtaken by a peculiar physical and emotional weakness. Suddenly, I couldn't process anything. Harry came and put his arm around me and led me back outside to sit in his car and wait for the police. We both seemed to have lost the powers of speech.

The police duly came within a half hour of Harry's call, surprisingly without Detective Eggers whom I had expected to be leading the pack. In fact, the lead person seemed to be Detective Lu, the one who had originally handled Martha's attack. We told him about the evening before, our dinner out, and my subsequent stay at Harry's due to the power outage. He ascertained that the house had thus been unoccupied from 6 PM Sunday until about 8 AM Monday. Yes. Except for two cats, very deft at hiding out. He went on to assume that the break-in had probably occurred after the power outage and before the power restoration, which would narrow the time from about 7:30 PM to 4:00 AM. That the invaders had taken advantage of the outage to by-pass the security apparatus seemed obvious. But the police had some feeling that perhaps the outage had not fully disabled the system, something about auxiliary generators providing some back-up, and so they wanted the contact information for my security people. When I gave it to Detective Lu, he nodded and said, good people, good service. He then gave me the name of a company that specialized in home-invasion clean-ups, in case I wanted to use them. His crime scene people remained doing what they do, but Lu left shortly after 9:30. He was a very quiet and courteous man and his manner was more reassuring to me than Detective Eggers had even been.

Harry and I spent what was left of the morning, after the CSI people left, doing our best to clean up. I wanted to avoid calling in an outside service if possible and thus further publicizing the break-in. In fact, most of what we had to do was just collect, bundle up, and bag the discards of my damaged property after photographing everything for the insurance people. We couldn't even begin to address the damage to the security panel covered with its glue-like substance, and of course I had already called the security people who promised to come in the afternoon to assess and begin repairs on the damaged system. I decided I could probably have my farm table sanded and refinished as the scratches, examined more closely, were mostly superficial. Since my refrigerator had been out of power for more than eight hours, I decided to throw out everything in it, which left Harry and I nothing but black coffee and some closeted soup to have for lunch. Harry insisted on going out to get some decent food and bring it back, and I took the opportunity while he was gone to call both Terry and Jared. Both were out, so I left messages. I admit I was uneasy while Harry was gone--although only for a scant half hour--alone in my now unprotected home. But when he came back with an armload of Chinese takeout, I decided it had been well worth the wait and the worry.

The aftermath to all this was the usual tedium: Dealings with the insurance people, another visit from Detective Lu later that day, a visit from Terry, the replacement of my computer, replacing my damaged possessions, and three days worth of repairs by the security people. Neither they nor the police told me whether or not they had been able to retrieve anything evidentiary from my system, and I didn't ask. I was exhausted, depressed, and more than happy to spend a few days at home, making coffee for the security repair guys and otherwise doing a whole lot of nothing. The bright spot was that while the system had been disarmed and damaged, all of the damage had been repairable or replaceable and the core of the system, as it was explained to me, was essentially in tact. The varnish that had been sprayed over the panel, the reason for which was never explained to me, was successfully removed by a mild solvent. I think everything was more or less insured and most everything could be replaced or repaired with only minimal cost to me. So, it was the old saw: Inconvenience, time and money, but thank God, no one was hurt. Even getting a new PC was reasonably easy, done in a few hours by my tech guy, although of course the hard drive was gone for good. Worst of all was re-setting my passwords for everything, everything. It took an entire morning. But most of the pictures I treasured were on my mobile phone, so I didn't have to face that loss and many of my computer files were backed up on an external server--also retrievable.

Jared at first wanted to come speeding back east to help oversee everything, but I convinced him that Terry and

Harry were helping me, that I was fine and healthy--if a bit dispirited--and that by Thursday, everything would be back to the way it had been, almost, except for some replacement purchases that would all get done the following week or later. So, somewhat reassured, Jared told me to call him every evening, just to check in, and I did.

The alone time I had during these two weeks, after settlements and repairs and while waiting for deliveries, gave me time to do what I don't do too often: think. I mean, I think all the time, but my thought processes, beyond the norm, tend toward analysis rather than introspection. I think more about what, when, where and why rather than how do I *feel* about this, what is my own emotional investment in these situations. I do analysis rather than psychoanalysis. But I thought that maybe it was time for me to start examining my feelings--what is it they say, "getting in touch with your feelings"--before they somehow crept up on me unawares. I kept trying to locate the predominant emotion. It was fear, of course, tempered by anger, but fear of what? Of intruders, murderers, thieves? Yes, but the more I tried to pin it down, the more I began to think that the fundamental fear came from the unknown. Why is all this happening to me? What invisible force is behind all these terrifying events--and what had I done, if anything, to trigger the unending disasters? They say that if your life seems to be moving out of control, you should examine *the new*, the elements recently introduced into your existence which no matter how innocent-seeming, might be a triggering force. The body in my shed had, of course, been, to put it mildly, the one "new" thing--but who put it there? Why? What had I let into my life or what had entered my life that was propelling the circumstances that created this essential fear in me? It seems that until I knew that, the only emotion I could be in touch with was fear of a threatening power about which I obviously had no knowledge and over which I had no control. It was a black hole, a vortex--and I really didn't see how getting in touch with this emotion was at all helpful--and was, in fact, more destructive than anything. We all fear the unknown, I thought, but for most people that doesn't put bodies in the shed or marauders in the breakfast room or a bullet in your friend's back. I kept coming back to "the new," and somewhere within these thoughts there kept appearing those attractive faces of Tad and Mariah and their dramatic new house on the hill. My new neighbors, so young and so chic--and so very "new."

16

The week after the break-in passed and by the following Monday, I was feeling that I had done all that needed to be done, all that I could do to return to normal, or what passed for normal during these distinctly non-normal times. During my nightly calls with Jared I would review my check-list of chores: Security System, repaired and working; insurance claims, filed and processed; replacement merchandise, ordered and starting to be delivered; nervous breakdown, averted--at least for now.

Detective Lu had made one more visit to my house on Friday, offering a brief and unproductive update that assured me that everything was being done to apprehend the criminals but sharing no information with me whatsoever that anything at all had been discovered as to their identities or their whereabouts. I didn't press the issue. I was feeling strangely passive, neither angry nor fearful anymore--just tired, I think, and almost resigned to this bizarre and chaotic series of events that populated my life. I established a rigid routine which I seldom altered. I thought of it as my grip on reality. I got up in the morning, fed the cats, made the coffee, made my bed, watched the news on TV, checked my mobile for mail and texts, ate a small breakfast, did chores, ate a small lunch, read, sewed, exercised by walking around my property or on my treadmill, started dinner, fed the cats again, had a cocktail, ate dinner, called Jared, watched TV some more, and went to bed. How tedious. I did occasionally chat with Martha on the phone, happy to know that she was making excellent progress, but I discouraged her from visiting me in my home, a place that I had begun to think of as the danger zone--fortified, protected--but very dangerous all the same.

Things went on this way for a few weeks until I had a strange call from Terrance the first week in March and then a hastily arranged visit. He advised me, as we sat at my newly re-finished breakfast table, that a warrant had been issued for my arrest and that I was to surrender myself to Detective Eggers the following morning.

PART TWO

17

The charges were confusing to me and no matter how carefully Terrance explained them, I seemed unable to grasp what "conspiracy to commit murder" could possibly mean. Conspiracy with whom? To murder a man with whom I had no connection? Why? What was the evidence? Terrance was doing more to calm me than to explain the legal niceties of my arrest, kept saying it was all a huge mistake and that I'd be arraigned--arraigned?--out on bail--bail?--and home by evening. I think I truly went into shock, couldn't think, could barely talk. Terrance was somehow able to get hold of Jared on the telephone and had a conversation with him that I couldn't hear, a conversation that seemed to go on forever.

We arrived at the local police station at 9:00 AM the next morning as previously arranged and were led to Eggers' office. There was a uniformed policeman there and surprisingly little was said. I was formally arrested, I guess "formally" is the appropriate term, read my rights, even though the lawyer to whom I was entitled was already there, and told I was being held for arraignment that afternoon at 1:00 PM. Presumably, Terrance had been aware of all this, made no objections and I, as told, remained totally quiet.

I was led to a little holding room, a cell, really, offered coffee which I declined, and then left there, to look at four walls. I had nothing except the clothes I was wearing, had been advised to wear no jewelry, and had left my purse in Terrence's car, promised its return after the bail hearing.

I have little recollection of the rest of that dreadful morning, and absolutely none of the arraignment. For whatever reason that I do not remember, the bail hearing was postponed, and I was transported in a van to the county jail in handcuffs. I vaguely recall Terrance patting my shoulder and saying it was all some bureaucratic mistake and that all would be straightened out the next morning. Meanwhile, I had to go through all the dehumanizing and undignified procedures involved with admitting me to jail and wound up at the end of the seemingly endless ordeal in a tiny cell, dressed in an orange jumpsuit, a garment that had heretofore been only the subject of jokes in my life--orange is the new black--and not a part of my wardrobe. I ate, or did not eat, a terrible dinner and spent an almost sleepless night on a pad they jokingly called a mattress, had my awful breakfast and my so-called exercise, and now here I sat, back in my cell, waiting only for what is next, with absolutely no idea of what that could possibly be--except bail, please God, bail.

18

Someone is fiddling with my cell door. I seem to have dozed off, but wake at the sound. I look at my wrist for the watch that is not there and see that someone is entering my cell. My heart jumps in fear. I am having trouble processing what's happening until a woman dressed in uniform, a kind of olive-khaki pants suit, takes my arm, rather gently, and says, come on dear, we're going to see your lawyer. I shake my head, blink, get to my feet, and walk beside her. She walks slowly to help me gain balance. We seem to walk forever, past other cells, down hallways, through security doors, through a room where women are playing ping pong or sitting in small groups, talking, orange clad women, like me, my sisters in infamy. My guard and I eventually arrive in another short hallway with three doors. One is opened by my guard onto a medium-sized conference room. I am ushered in and placed in a chair at a conference table. My guard asks if I would like some coffee and I answer, as if from a trance, yes please, black, an automatic response. She leaves, comes back a few minutes later with a china mug, not a Styrofoam cup, three-quarters filled with coffee that does not smell like instant. It is quite hot. She smiles a half smile and sits behind me in a chair against the outer wall. There is a clock in this room and it says 10:30. She says nothing, nor do I. We sit. We wait.

Ten minutes later, Terrance enters the room with Eggers, with two other men I don't know, have never seen before, and with a fifth man who is, I am certain, Timmy Mooks, clean-shaven as I had glimpsed him behind the wheel that night in San Diego, dressed in a grey suit, wearing his glasses, a straight-eyed Timmy. My mouth opens and for some unaccountable reason, I start to cry--not loud crying or sobbing, just tears running down my face. I realize that I fear Timmy Mooks, always have, and that his presence here is somehow far more terrifying to me than it was in his odd Spanish villa or even in his car driving down a dark street at midnight. Someone hands me a tissue, Terrance pats my shoulder, and the crazy silent charade proceeds. The men seat themselves and my guard quietly exits the room.

Some of the men clear their throats, some open zip cases and take out documents, but only Timmy Mooks looks at me. I look back and then down. I will look at my lap and not at anyone for the moment.

It is Eggers who finally speaks. He begins by apologizing to me, stammering a bit, asking for my understanding and my help, help with what he doesn't say. He tells me that the gentlemen who have accompanied Mr. Hannity, my lawyer, and himself to this meeting are all federal agents from the Department of Homeland Security, the DHS. He doesn't enlighten me much about anything, but introduces me to the men whom he calls Mr. X, Mr. Y, and of course Mr. Z, whom I might remember as Mr. Timothy Mooks from our previous meetings? Oh yes. I remember. I nod. I look briefly at Mr. Z, aka Timmy.

I am like a girl at a surprise party, waiting for someone to tell me what the party is for and why I seem to be the feted guest.

The explanations are limited, "need to know" they say. I have been "arrested" so to speak, one of them says, partly for my own protection (to be placed in federal custody) and as part of an ongoing investigation and a complicated take down. They plan to remove me from this facility (the county jail), keep me in protective custody, and install an agent in my home to take my place. This agent will be released from the county jail this morning on bail, under my name, returned to my home to reside there, disguised well enough, they hope, to sufficiently resemble me from a distance, inside a car. I will appear as myself at the bail hearing shortly but then be taken secretly from this place to a safe location until their operation is concluded. This will require a disguise and absolute secrecy.

I am now like an actress in a movie and, I think, am in a state of mild shock,

I look at Terrance and he nods and Mr. X takes the cue and tells me that Mr. Hannity has been read in on the situation to the degree possible and concurs that this plan will assist our investigation and provide absolute safety for me while it is ongoing.

I ask where I am going. They say, to a safe place. I ask who I am going with, they say that the lady guard who escorted me this morning and Mr. Z will be my initial escorts. I ask for how long, they say they don't know, hopefully not long at all. I ask who will feed my cats, they say the agent in place (she loves cats, they say; but my cats won't love her, I think, no matter how much she resembles me from a distance).

With that, our little meeting seems to be over. Terrance offers me brief assurances, says he has been in touch with Jared, and says I can trust that this is all for the best. I am told to say nothing during the bail hearing, to let my lawyer speak for me and then to go with my guard afterwards. I nod, in a daze, I squeeze Terrance's arm, the men leave and my guard returns. We make the long return walk to my cell where I sit and wait for a lunch call and then for my bail hearing.

The lunch is awful and the bail hearing is short. Bail is proposed, is granted, and Terrance goes to pay it as I am removed from the courtroom by my guard. She is a very medium woman--height, weight, ethnicity. She is possibly about forty, has short brown hair, even features, looks like a thousand other women. Her voice is low and she rarely speaks. She escorts me to an elevator I have not been in before and takes me down as far as the elevator will go. We exit it into an underground parking garage. She leads me to a black SUV with tinted windows, asks me to lie down on the passenger seat in the back, and cover myself with the blanket that is on the seat. I want to ask where Terrance is, but I suspect he will soon be escorting the fake-me agent from the courthouse, taking her back to my home and to my cats and to my life while I, I am being protected--why and from whom, I apparently do not have the "need to know."

We drive, from what I can tell, first through the city streets beyond the county jail, and then onto a parkway of some sort as we no longer stop for traffic lights, increase our speed, encounter less traffic noise. Eventually, we slow down, make a few turns, drive a bit further, stop, and then seem to coast downhill, coming to a gradual stop. I estimate that we have been driving for perhaps a half hour and try to make a little map in my head of all the places within a half hour of the county jail. Too many, too confusing. My guard turns off the engine and then tells me, softly, that we are at our destination and that I can shed the blanket and get out of the car. When I do, I see we are in another subterranean parking garage. I follow the guard to an elevator. I don't see what button she pushes but we seem to go up a rather long way before the elevator stops, the doors open, and we are let out into what looks like an office suite of some sort. We are standing in a reception area where there is one unoccupied and relatively empty desk in the center of the floor, and an arrangement of chairs and couches against the walls. Everything looks very new, very modern, very efficient, no frills, no pictures on the walls, the carpet a medium grey color, the furnishings chrome and black. There are glass doors to hallways on the left and right, but no windows in this room, nothing at all to show where we might be. So I ask the guard--first, what I'm to call her, and next, where are we? She says her name is Emily, which I doubt, but will call her, and she tells me that we are in one of their offices (the feds?) and that we are here to prepare me for travel to the safe house, our eventual destination.

She leads me through the glass doors to the left and we walk down the hallway to a door at the end. She punches some kind of code into a small panel on the wall to unlock this door and as we go in, I'm stunned to see that we are in what looks decidedly like a salon, a woman's beauty salon, a very chic one, with all the expected accoutrements. Emily intuits my surprise and simply says, we need to tweak your appearance a bit and get you ready to travel. I know next to nothing about the Department of Homeland Security, what comprises it and what it does, but I have to say, although deeply in shock and feeling rather like Alice through the Looking Glass, I am in a very odd way, enormously impressed. This is better than a Bond film, I say to Emily, and for the first time since she walked into my cell this morning, Emily smiles.

Apparently, I am to have some transformative procedures. I am first given a choice between a wig or a hair cut and color. While I am loathe to have my hair cut, the thought of being imprisoned in the skill cap of a wig is even more disheartening, so I chose the cut and color option. I want to ask why, but I know this will be futile. While I am being so unlovingly protected, I am also their prisoner, at their mercy, and both Emily and I know that. Through a far door, a man enters and motions me to one of the client chairs in front of a gilt-framed mirror. He wraps the requisite black beauty cape around my shoulders and begins to run his fingers through my hair, hair that has not worn well throughout my captivity and is now disheveled and dry. After a few minutes and a brief conversation with Emily, he wheels a cart over and begins mixing hair colors. And so it begins.

After a few hours, I am done. My hair is cropped short, a beautiful cut, really, and colored brown with a few highlights; my makeup is classic, but I now have bright red lips, a color I have rejected for my entire adult life. Contact lenses have been provided so that I now have brown instead of green eyes, and over my eyes are a new pair of eyeglasses, large, with dark tortoise shell frames. To me, I look like me, a freaky me, but me. But Emily and my stylist seem pleased with the results and tell me it's time to go shopping. After another hour in a large room filled with racks and racks of women's clothing and tables on which are piles of lingerie, I am "outfitted." The clothing is chosen for me, far from anything I would have chosen for myself, but follows a theme: It is clothing designed to subtly alter my physical shape. When I am led to a small dressing room and given what will be my "travel outfit" to put on, I find myself dressing in a white round neck sweater and a black pantsuit, the jacket padded out. The shoes have lifts which add a few inches to my height. So, I am taller and fatter. But the clothing fits, is reasonably comfortable, and the shoes are wedge-styled which makes walking in them quite easy, regardless of their height. I am careful as I dress to keep my hair and made-up face in tact, and replace the huge glasses when I am done. I step outside the dressing room and both Emily and my stylist nod approval, as does the ubiquitous Timmy Mooks who has apparently joined them while I completed my transformation. Timmy tells me I look "perfect," his word, and how would I like some dinner?

And so we go, Timmy, Emily and me, down the elevator to another floor, down another hall, and into a small dining room, another amazing surprise. It is a lovely intimate room, furnished with dark mahoghany dining furniture, capped with a glowing chandelier filled with small, bright lights but, of course, no windows. Three places are set with fine china and crystal, and there seems to be some sort of buffet set up on one of the side tables. Timmy leads the way, taking a plate, offering one to me, and then begins to serve himself from the buffet. I discover selections of appetizers, salads, and two entrees--fish or sliced beef. I discover that after all of the day's shocks and changes, I am still ravenous, and am able to eat a smoked salmon appetizer, a small Caesar salad, and some rare sliced beef and beans almondine. Timmy solicitously offers wine, and I have a glass of Pinot Noir which I feel sinking into my cells and relaxing me. Our talk is limited and desultory. Timmy assures me that the fake me agent has successfully returned to my home with no issues and assures me that she will take good care--of my house and of my cats. I am not particularly reassured but at least happy to know there has been no more violence--shooting or looting. Timmy also tells me we will be leaving for a small private airstrip very soon, and will take a short flight to the safe house that has been prepared for me. I am surprised. A flight? Just to get y-y-you away from the area, ahem, the action, Timmy says, stuttering slightly. As ever, I don't protest. In for a penny, in for a pound I say and both Timmy and Emily smile at me, like little fake parents indulging a bratty child.

I am reluctant to leave this charming room, the food, the comfort of the wine, and face one more ride in the black SUV, under the blanket, but I refresh my lips with the bright red lipstick provided for me and I go and I do, and we are soon, all three, standing inside an airplane hanger, waiting for a small jet plane to taxi up close and take us on board. Here we go, I think. The wild blue yonder. Where do we go? Well, no "need to know" that. At least, not yet.

19

I wake up suddenly. Still in the airplane. The lighting is dimmed, the flight smooth, the soft leather passenger seats so comfortable that I am drawn back down to sleep again. But I shake my head, try to wake. Did Timmy slip something into my wine to make me this drowsy, I think, but then considering the events of the day, I seem to have enough reasons to be exhausted without the help of drugs. I look again at my empty wrist. No one has given me my watch or a replacement, so I have no idea of the time or of how long we've been aloft. I keep guessing about time, but have few if any prompts to help me out. It is dark outside the plane, so I know that wherever we are, in whatever time zone, it is night. This is not enlightening in the least.

I look around the cabin and see Timmy--or, at least, Timmy's legs--stretched out in the aisle a few rows ahead of me. The plane has only ten rows of the *luxe* leather seats, spaced generously, two on each side of the aisle. In the front of the cabin is a small lounge area with semi-circular couches on either side, a low lounge table in the middle. Emily sits on one of these lounges, her feet on the table, leafing slowly through a magazine to which she does not seem to be paying much attention. She still wears her olive drab uniform, but has unbuttoned the jacket. The door to the cockpit is closed behind her and on we fly. As there seems little to stay awake for, I allow myself to drift softly back to my dreamless sleep, looking stupidly, once more, at my empty wrist, to discover no time, no time at all.

I am next awakened by the simultaneous change in engine sounds, the brightening of the cabin lights, and a loud speaker announcement: Prepare for landing. So, wherever we are going, we are almost there. I straighten up, click my seat upright, fasten my seat belt, and blink a few times as my eyes adjust. Timmy stands, stretches, looks down the aisle and, seeing that I am prepared as instructed, gives me a thumbs up and returns to his seat. Emily abandons the lounge and takes a seat across the aisle from Timmy. All set.

Soon I feel us descending and banking to the left. It is a long, slow descent but eventually, runway lights appear, flash close below, and then our wheels are down and we are landed. No one comes on the speaker to welcome us to Boise or Topeka or Tampa or to wherever we are, however. We just taxi on and eventually come abreast of another hangar, not unlike the one we left from, taxi to a stop, and then prepare to de-plane. As I stand, I find that I am incredibly stiff and wriggle and bend in order to dislodge the worst of the kinks. Seeing this, Timmy asks if I am OK and I tell him I am just stiff, will be fine in a minute or two. The door to the cockpit remains shut, but the exit door opens automatically. I smell fresh air and as it drifts into the cabin, it seems warmish and humid. I cannot see ground crew from my position, but hear the ladder being pushed to the plane's door and hear rumblings below from the cargo hatch, so apparently we have greeters. A small van appears, the ubiquitous black SUV with tinted windows variety, more rumbles--our luggage being unloaded, I suspect--while Timmy stands at the door of the aircraft with his hand raised, motioning me to stay where I am. Soon he beckons me forward, takes my arm and guides me down the stairs, and then walks me to the van. This time, I am allowed to sit in the passenger seat, no blanket cover. Emily gets in the back and Timmy takes the driver's seat and we are off. The ground crew and flight crew remain invisible, and soon we are driving beyond the hangar, down a fenced-in airport side road, and finally through gates and onto some other road, heading somewhere.

Timmy is quiet for a while and then tells me that we are on an island. He says he is driving us to a secluded retreat--sounds almost luxurious--where we will remain until it is safe to return. Well accustomed to the rules of the game by now, I ask no questions that I know will go politely unanswered, make no comments, show no interest. I look around me. We are driving on a road lined with live oaks and moss and I think we are perhaps on an island off the east coast of the Carolinas or Georgia. But I don't guess out loud. Wherever we are, it is dark and quiet, and pleasantly warm-ish, although not hot, not the tropics. The SUV hums quietly along this lonely road and then turns into something that looks like a long driveway. We turn right and then left and emerge in a cul de sac at the end of which is a singular house. It appears to be a large, plantation-style cottage, with a screened-in verandah surround, a few dim lights in the windows. Timmy parks the SUV in front, gives Emily the keys, tells her to go on in and that he'll be in shortly with the luggage.

Emily and I open the screen door, cross the verandah past comfortable rockers, little tables and hanging ferns, and then after she unlocks the front door, we enter the cottage. It seems slightly air conditioned as it is less humid inside. We stand in a spacious foyer that runs to the back of the cottage, has a large fan slowly rotating overhead, and has a wide staircase to the left. To the right is a sitting room furnished in plantation rattan, driftwood grey in color with bright cushions and throw pillows, a large straw rug in the middle of the floor in front of a fireplace over which hangs a monster flat-screen TV. To the left is a dining room, furnished in white wicker, the glass-topped table adorned with glass hurricane shades over white candles. An open door in the back wall of the dining room shows a kitchen beyond, gleaming white cabinets and white marble counters from what little I can see. Very nice. Standard three-million dollar vacation home, I'm guessing.

Timmy lumbers into the foyer with our luggage, closes and locks the door behind him, fiddles with a wall panel which I assume to be the security system, and then turns to look at us. I think now, he says, that we have all earned a drink, small smile. He goes into the dining room, takes some glasses from the shelf over the wet bar, and asks what we'll have, and I find myself saying Scotch, please, a response that startles me more that it startles Timmy. But somehow the idea of sipping whiskey and feeling its burn is exactly what I need at this moment and, without comment, Timmy locates Scotch among the collection of bottles and pours both himself and me three fingers of the amber liquid into lovely cut glass tumblers. Emily opts for a Coke. We take our drinks to the living room, flop on the sofas which are surprisingly soft and comfortable, and then just look around and take stock. Timmy says he hasn't been here before, but understands that upstairs there are four bedrooms, three with en suite baths, so that we can decide who gets what room after we drink for a while, and then he will distribute the luggage accordingly. It's good to know that we will each have out own bath and feeling good about that, I sip my Scotch and feel as relaxed as I suppose anyone could ever feel under the circumstances.

As we sit and sip, Timmy enlightens me a little, apparently feeling that now that we have reached "safety," my need to know might be moderately satisfied.

He refers to their target as an international criminal enterprise that has been under investigation for three years by various branches of the DHS. He does not identify the crime. He indicates that Mr. Arthur, aka the body in my shed, had inadvertently become involved with some members of this enterprise and had to be eliminated by them. Unfortunately, this "elimination," murder, had been bungled and, as a result, Mr. Arthur had wound up in my shed. He doesn't elaborate. This, in turn, brought me, also inadvertently, into the "big picture" and rather than allowing these "inconvenient events" to interfere with or detract from their ongoing investigation in any way, they decided on this current course of action. Could I see that? Well, yes, sort of, I say. And I appreciate your concern for my safety, I continue, as shocking as all this has been to my system. Emily comments that I've been a brick. I'm surprised to hear her chime in and even more surprised at the compliment. I'm not sure about the brick part, I say, but my faith in Terrance is absolute--and really, his reassurance is what has kept me going. We drink in silence for a while and then begin going about the business of arrival, selecting rooms, distributing luggage, and getting unpacked. And I am finally entitled to the time, as there is a clock in the bedroom I select which tells me it is 11:37 PM.

20

The bedroom I have selected is not the largest, but seems the coziest to me. Timmy has christened it "the rose room" because it is painted in a deep rose color and the wall behind the four-poster bed is papered in a rose-print pattern. There is a chaise lounge in one corner covered in pale pink velvet. The furniture is all bleached pine. There is a small chest with an electric kettle and the makings of coffee and tea on top. The cabinet part is actually a refrigerator stocked with juice, coke, and "healthy snacks." There is a large flat screen TV on the wall opposite the bed and the small bathroom is all dazzling white tile with pink and white towels and mats, fully equipped with toiletries. A white terry toweling robe hangs on the back of the bathroom door partially covering a full-length mirror. I catch part of my reflection in that mirror and am momentarily stunned. I have managed to forget my "new look," and for just a second think: Who is that lady with the short brown stylish haircut and the big shoulders? But she is me, for a while, and I just shake my head and get over this strange doppelganger.

I unpack the wardrobe we have selected, limited and practical: Another pants suit (also suitably padded) in lightweight camel hair wool, two sweaters, two track suits, some underwear, a white cotton nightgown, slippers, sneakers. I feel slightly relieved that this limited assortment of clothing bodes a short stay, for which I am grateful and on which I pin my hopes for an early departure.

I brush my teeth after I put on my nightgown and suddenly am bone weary, the day and the Scotch finally catching up with me. The bed is comfortable, the puffy quilt warm, and I fall suddenly and totally into a sound and dreamless sleep.

The morning light wakens me and I am astonished to see that it is a little after 8:00 AM, very late for me to wake. But after my day of escape and with no kitties to remind me that it's breakfast time, I am not surprised that I have slept in. I just lie there under the warm quilt, rehearsing for a moment the events of the previous day, luxuriating in the fact that exile that I am, the day that looms ahead will be undemanding, restful. I wish I had brought along some books, but am gratified to see a small bookshelf on the wall that contains some readable titles.

I rise and walk to the window. A window! Daylight! Delightful, although there is not much to see out my window. The roof of the verandah runs immediately below it and beyond is a small lawn backed by the ubiquitous live oaks which make a kind of irregular small forest that slopes down into what appears to be swampy ground, patches of still water visible. Not totally unexpectedly, I see Timmy Mooks out walking the perimeter of the lawn doing his guard duty, I suspect. He has changed his suit this morning for khaki pants and a black sweater and I find that I am beginning to actually feel a certain fondness for Timmy. I never asked if he were dispatched to San Diego to follow me and I won't--because he won't answer and because, oddly, I don't want to embarrass him. I also wonder if the name Timmy Mooks, which seems to suit him, is actually his real name. I doubt it, but he will always be Timmy Mooks to me, regardless.

After I dress in one of the track suits, navy with white stripes, totally unpadded, thank goodness, I have some juice and coffee. I hear no people sounds and wonder where Emily is. I wonder if I will be summoned, eventually, or if I'm "free" to roam the house. I have no intention of going outside, although the sun is out and it looks like a pretty day. But I sense that one does not poke her nose out of a "Safe House."

So, I put on my bright red lipstick, ever ready to keep up my end of the deal, brush my obedient short hair, and exit the rose room for parts below. I find both Emily and Timmy in the kitchen, eating cereal and drinking coffee. Emily has abandoned her uniform and is clad in a track suit similar to mine only dark green in color. We exchange morning greetings, and comment on the sun as I help myself to some cereal and more coffee.

As I eat my cereal, crunchy granola, I ask Timmy how long he thinks we'll be here in our svelte plantation cottage. He smiles, shrugs, and then, surprisingly, again elaborates a little. He tells me that the *operation*, as he calls it, has been lengthy and complicated, with national and international implications, but he thinks it "verges on solution" within days. And then he smiles, to let me know that's all I'm getting. I switch subjects and ask him about the house rules governing my stay, our stay, whatever, and he says he thinks it best if I confine myself to the house and the verandah. I am happy about access to the verandah as I am feeling slightly claustrophobic--and also aware that the sun is warming as the morning brightens, that it might be a pretty day. Even a stroll around the limited space of the verandah sounds almost like freedom, and so I plan my little walk for mid-morning. Emily suggests we might also lunch out there and, about 1:00 PM, we do.

I sit in the rocker while Emily serves--a chef's salad with iced tea and some warm rolls. She talks about the weather, the marsh behind the cottage, her cat (she knows I have cats), and then offers dessert. But I refuse. The lunch has been perfect, as is, I say. We sit for a while as the sun has moved around to where we are and the warmth is pleasant. I feel myself begin to doze as I notice Emily starting to clear up. I snap awake and say, oh no, you cooked, I'll clean up, and gather the dishes and glasses, putting them on the tray that Emily has carried them out on. I bring everything into the kitchen, run a sink full of warm soapy water, and wash up our few things. I find a cloth, dry everything, and by opening several cabinets, locate where everything belongs. I yawn and decide I could use a little nap, even given my long night's sleep, so I go to the door and shout out to Emily that I'm retiring to my room for a nap. And then I go upstairs, fold back the coverlet, lie down, and am almost instantly asleep.

I am wakened roughly by Timmy shaking me and then putting a finger to his lips, signaling my silence. He walks around the room, checks in the bathroom, shuts the bedroom door, and sits down next to me. He asks me, sotto voice, if I know where Emily is or when had I last seen her.

I recount to him our lunch, my doing dishes, then calling out to her that I was going up for a nap, about two o'clock, I think. Did she answer, he asks? I don't remember, I say. I'm not sure--but maybe not. OK, he says. We're leaving, Can you pack in five minutes. I'm shocked but I nod and say yes, I can. I'll be back in five, he says, as I rush to get the suitcase and start throwing things into it while Timmy exits. I hear a click and think maybe the door locks from the outside? But I am too busy getting my things into the case to check. Timmy returns, locks us into the bedroom, and tells me we are exiting through the window, across the verandah roof, and down a small ladder he's put in place. Can I do that? Yes, yes, I think so, and we go. Climbing out the window is easy and walking down the slightly pitched roof of the verandah is ok. Timmy precedes me down the rather wobbly ladder slanted against the roof and then stands at the bottom, steadying it while I climb down, thanking God that I am wearing the sneakers and not those tricky wedgies.

At the foot of the ladder a vehicle is waiting, not the black SUV in which we arrived, but a kind of jeep-truck looking vehicle that says Range Rover across the back. Timmy points me to the passenger seat, gathers up my suitcase and the ladder and thrusts these into the back of the vehicle. He gets into the driver's seat and says, briefly, Plan B, and we begin to drive away from the cottage, through the woods behind it and not down the front drive. I am silent--because I am panicked, because I don't know what's happened to Emily, because Timmy looks demented, and because I know he won't say a word to me until we are well into the execution of Plan B, whatever that might be.

The drive through the woods is terrifying. We seem

to be barely missing collisions with the trees and as we reach the swamp land, we make dangerous turns to avoid its traps--still water, mud patches, dead wood sticking up from the boggy places. Timmy drives relentlessly on and finally, finally, we reach something resembling a trail--not a road, but at least a solid, dirt-packed byway on which the vehicle has some stability. But this is even more terrifying in its way, because once on relatively solid ground, Timmy accelerates and the speed he reaches is almost more frightening than the obstacle course we have just left behind. I realize that I am gripping the passenger side handle with both hands, painfully, that my hands are growing numb, and I force myself to let go, to place my hands on either side of me on the seat for balance, and to take very deep breaths the way my yoga coach at the gym once told me to do.

I don't know how long we are on the dirt road. I still don't have my watch and don't even think to look for a clock in our Rover, but eventually, maybe a half hour later, or more, we reach a paved road, and Timmy stops. He backs the vehicle into a clearing just off the paved road, turns off the engine, and says. OK, now we wait. For what, I say? For help, I hope, he answers, none too convincingly. It is getting dark. I look around, but there is nothing to see. There is the paved road in front of us, bushes around us, trees beyond that. I can hear soft animal noises, the occasional flutter of leaves, and start to relax before I notice that Timmy is holding a gun. It's in his right hand which is relaxed in his lap, but it's a gun. I don't say a word. Cat has definitely got my tongue.

So we wait and we wait. And eventually, we see what I presume to be headlights from a car coming down the paved road, from my left. Timmy straightens up, moves both hands holding the gun now to the top of the steering wheel until the headlights become a car--or, no, a black SUV that stops on the road, in front of our vehicle. Timmy cracks the window and a voice from the SUV says Tim, zero-one-zero, and I see Timmy visibly relax, place the gun in his belt, and then say to me, show time. He exits the Rover and motions for me to do the same. He leaves the keys in the ignition, gets my case from the back, and guides me to the SUV. Someone gets out, Timmy and I and my bag get in the back seat. The driver of the SUV moves out quickly and the man left behind heads for the Range Rover, and pulls it out behind us. He follows for a while, then veers off a side road and leaves Timmy and me to travel on with our driver, unescorted.

Eventually, we are at an air field which looks like the same one we came in on yesterday and quickly after that, we are on what looks like the same aircraft we were on yesterday. We board, buckle up, and are wheels up in a dizzyingly brief time. After we level off at altitude and are told by the same computer voice that we can unfasten our seat belts and move freely about the cabin, Timmy looks at me and says in an exaggerated cartoon voice: Whew. He moves to the lounge area and without even asking, pours us both a stiff drink, Scotch I discover as he hands it to me.

OK, he says. We don't know if Emily will make it. She was found pretty badly beaten, unconscious, but they got her to hospital quickly and she has a fighting chance, or so they tell us. She was apparently snatched from the verandah some time after your lunch, managed to dial for emergency help after her beating and before she lost consciousness.

Our people were able to get to her pretty quickly. Why you weren't snatched, we don't know, unless their surveillance was poor and they hadn't seen you or they saw you and didn't recognize you. That seems somewhat improbable, so perhaps you weren't the target after all. We don't know. We'll find out, but obviously, we had to move you. So, on we go. Timmy looks at me over the rim of his glass and all I can think to say is thank you and I'm praying for Emily. She has a lovely big yellow cat who loves her.

Timmy then surprises me by telling me what our current destination is. I am surprised at how free he is becoming with information. We're not going too far this time, he says, just to a little island in the Florida Keys. I'm afraid the accommodations will not be as salubrious as those of the plantation cottage, just a little out-of-the-way motel, no longer in business for the general public. But, he adds, it's on the beach, a rather nice beach, with some palm trees, so perhaps you won't mind too much. I tell him that I'm sure I'll be fine, am just happy we keep heading south, away from the cold. I want to add that I hope this stay won't include a mad drive through a swamp, but I don't say that as it strikes me that it will sound ungrateful. After all, Timmy was risking his own life and limbs as well as mine, and I know that.

And so we fly on and eventually get the seat belt sign and begin to circle into yet another landing on another island. I like islands, frequently vacation on them, mostly in the Caribbean: the Dominican, Bermuda, San Juan, Nassau, St. Croix, all so lovely and balmy, surrounded by the gem-like blue waters. Once, I went to Madeira--a Portuguese island off the coast of Africa--which was also lovely, but with strange flora that endlessly attracted me, big trees with blooms that shed a cottony substance, shrubs with scant laves but huge yellow blooms that shed blood red veins at their hearts. The notable product was wine, of course, and a trip to a winery taught me more than I ever needed to know about Madeira wine--but the free samples were lovely and of course I wound up buying a case for shipment home. The wine reminded me of that lovely island, long after I left it. So, landing on yet another island did not seem at all strange to me. It seemed comfortable--although not quite a vacation.

I was expecting a kind of roach motel given Timmy's disclaimers, but when we arrived, was happily surprised that our destination was more like a small resort than a tacky motel. It was Spanish in style, pinkish stucco with red tiled roofs, with a small two-storied building in the center of what were a collection of small bungalows and not a string of attached rooms. The grounds were dotted with small ground-level lanterns, with paths leading to each of the bungalows which each had relatively lush gardens, flowering plants and tall palms surrounding them. It was enchanting, really. Even in the darkness, I could see that it was a bit run down, but it was still surprisingly charming. I could hear surf and so Timmy's promise that we'd be on a beach was fulfilled. We by-passed the main building and headed to a small cluster of three cottages toward the rear left, partially hidden from view. Timmy took me down a short gravel path to the center cottage, unlocked the door, and preceded me inside with my case.

I ducked a low hanging palm branch and followed him inside. The cottage was an open-space style, one large room subdivided by various curved arches into a sitting room, galley kitchen, and sleep space--a bed built into an alcove in one wall. A door to one side suggested a lavatory. The furnishings were Spanish style, very colorful, with two tall, ornately carved chairs standing at a kitchen counter, some wrought iron lamps and deco items. It was clean and neat and smelled of something musky--and was delightful. Oh, Timmy, I said. How lovely.

He set my case on the bed and said he'd leave me to unpack and look around. If I were to find anything that wasn't there that I might need, I was to let him know and he'd do his best to get it for me. He said we'd be taking meals at the main inn, so to eliminate those from my consideration.

The sleep area had a built-in closet and drawers which easily accommodated my limited wardrobe. The lavatory and kitchen seemed well equipped--and after my inspection tour, I could think of nothing to ask Timmy for. There were the default coffee, tea, juice, and coke supplies, as well as some snacks. There was even a small liquor cabinet stocked with airplane sized bottles of wine and spirits. There was a TV set and a clock-radio, but, I noticed, no telephone. I'd mention this to Timmy. If I were to be inhabiting this little hacienda alone, would I not need some means of communicating out? In case? And that thought gave me a small shiver. I had really wanted to ask Timmy all day how we had been discovered at the plantation cottage, the so-called safe house (not so safe), but I was afraid to think about that--or that it might happen again here on another supposedly "safe" island. And I was pretty sure Timmy would give me the *de rigueur* "we don't know" answer.

After my inspection tour, I decided to unpack, to see what, in my hasty departure, I had left out of my case but was pleased to see that I had managed to get everything in during that frantic five minutes of packing. I put all away, and sat down on a comfortable couch with a two-year old copy of *Vogue*, to wait for Timmy.

21

And I waited. And waited.

After almost an hour had passed and I had made every possible excuse for what was delaying the usually prompt Timmy, panic started to set in. I took a few deep breaths and began to consider my options, all the while sure that Timmy would be tapping on the door momentarily. What could I do? If something had happened to Timmy, should I go out and look for him on the argument that he might be lying ill or injured and in need of assistance? Wouldn't he have a way of summoning help if that were the case? And, in light of our circumstances and Emily's fate, wasn't it far more reasonable to believe that if anything had "happened" to Timmy, it was purposeful and nefarious and that I might be walking into danger if I left the cottage? Or, would I be a sitting duck, courting danger, if I stayed? If someone had done harm to Timmy and intended harm to me, it was really too late to do anything, wasn't it?

I had no mobile phone and there was no phone in the cottage. My phone probably resided with my "double" back at my house so that anyone who might be tracking me would find my phone where it was supposed to be--with "me" (not me). The story was that I was given bail but placed on house arrest with an ankle monitor, allowed no contact with anyone except immediate family.

I dithered and dithered. Time passed--it was now after 11:00 PM--and still I did nothing. *When in doubt, do nothing.* But one thought occurred to me as I sat there, a thought that gave me some small comfort: If something terrible had happened to Timmy and the authors of his fate were also after me, they'd have found me by now. I was sitting in the only lighted cottage here and although it was nestled behind the main building, it would have taken only five minutes of reconnaissance to discover it. I did go around turning off all but one small light in the sleeping area, but it was now considerably more than an hour since it would have been reasonable to expect Timmy's return, and so if someone had wanted to find me, they already would have. I just had to believe that. I had to wait. That's what I had to do. Wait and hope.

As much as I never would have believed I could, I started to get sleepy sometime after 1:00 AM. I got a pillow and a small coverlet, took off my sneakers, and stretched out on the couch. I must have fallen asleep shortly thereafter, because the next thing I knew I was startled awake by a slant of sunshine coming through the blinds. Sunrise? I blinked awake, momentarily disoriented, and then slowly became aware of where I was and what was happening, and I bolted upright on the couch and frantically looked around. Everything appeared to be exactly as it had been when I dozed off. I groggily made my way to the small fridge and got out a little bottle of orange juice and slugged it down, desperately thirsty and in need of some sugar energy. The first thing I did after that was to put my sneakers back on--some instinct of flight, I suppose--and then I decided to see what I could see out of the windows. While the ray of sun that woke me signaled daylight outside, the cottage was still in relative darkness. There was one large bay window in the sitting room area, a smaller window in the kitchen, and one of frosted glass in the lavatory, that was it. The two usable windows gave me only a partial view of the cottage's surroundings and a totally uninformative partial view at that. Everything was quiet, the palm leaves swayed slightly in the morning breeze, no human form was visible, and no sounds penetrated inside except the trilling of some morning birds. Still, quiet, empty. I tried to remember if I had heard anything after Timmy left last night. Voices? A motor? Scuffling? But I could remember none of these.

Hungry, as we had eaten nothing last night, I first made myself some coffee for caffeine energy, and then discovered some so-called health bars among the snacks, one of which sufficed for me as cereal. I knew after I had eaten I was going to have to go out and look around. I knew I could not simply sit endlessly in this lovely little bungalow--waiting for my fate or Godot or whatever was in store for me. And I reasoned that the sooner I went to explore, the better. Perhaps the other inhabitants of this island, if there were any, were not yet up and about. Stupid, I guess, but I couldn't think of anything smart. I could survive for quite a while on the supplies in the cottage, maybe a week, couldn't I? But then what? You have to leave sometime. No time like the present.

I should have saved myself the worry. I quietly left the cottage, re-traced our steps of the night before. Nothing, nobody. Not even the golf cart in which we had traveled here from the airstrip. I tried the door of the main building. It was unlocked. Inside, a pleasant, if slightly shabby, reception area--a counter, a few couches and tables with lamps. Nobody. Beyond that was a small dining room with maybe ten tables and next to that, a kitchen that looked newly outfitted. Beyond the dining room windows--palm trees and then the beach. I checked the kitchen for food and there seemed to be enough for several days for more than one person--eggs, bacon, milk, bread, salads, deli meats, frozen chicken, steaks, chops, fish, fresh fruits and vegetables and sundry other edibles. I took a Clementine from a bowl on the counter, peeled it, ate some, and asked myself how much further a field was I willing to go. I was hesitant to climb the stairs of this building to find four empty guest bedrooms--which I was sure were what was there--although in the end I did and was right. Was I willing to walk to the beach, exposing myself to anyone watching? Maybe. Where, after all, was I? Who knew I was here, here alone? Would stalking the beach tell me anything? Probably not, but I wanted to have some idea of the size of this island and of its proximity to other land masses. I knew the bungalows were reasonably close to the airstrip we had landed on, as the ride from there to La Playa (the name of this place, discovered this morning carved into a wooden sign) was a very short drive. I had thoughts of going to the airstrip to seek help, but could not be certain that anyone was actually there or, if anyone were, whether they'd be friend or foe.

I decided to go to the beach, but stay among the palm trees that bordered it, and find out as much about the island's perimeter as was possible--or maybe find a convenient boat that I could row to the mainland, if there even was a mainland within my rowing capacity.

I soon discovered that the beach, at both ends, ended in rocky shoals, that La Playa was set in what was a cove, and that in order to walk the island's perimeter, one would have to do some rock climbing and swimming. So, forget that. There was a rather large dock at the far end of the beach, but it was empty of any boats or anything else.

So I walked in the direction of where I thought the airstrip might be and found it, just an airstrip, a small shack at one end, some kind of metal tower at the other, all apparently uninhabited. I was still shielding myself behind the trees bordering the strip when I heard a noise, sensed some motion, and was suddenly bumped into by a large and friendly dog, a dog! His tail was wagging and he was attempting to put his front paws up on my shoulders, a big fuzzy yellow dog--maybe a golden? I laughed out loud and cried. Hey, fella, I said, how are you! At the sound of my voice, he started to run in circles around me letting out small yips. He seemed as happy to have met me as I was to see him. Dogs lived with people, right? So where were his people--and who were they? International criminals or government agents don't travel with dogs, do they? But Timmy had implied that this island was uninhabited.

I waited for the dog to stop his circling and yipping, still hoping that he'd settle down and then start going someplace that I could follow him to. Home? I asked him tentatively? Like, Lassie go home? But the command apparently meant nothing to him except his happiness that I was paying him attention. He stood beside me, still wagging his big fluffy tail, and did not move. As I started to walk a bit, he started to follow me. No, I thought. Wrong. You walk. I'll follow. But when I stopped, he stopped. And so I finally started back to La Playa with Fella trotting along happily beside me and me thinking that maybe he was my new Timmy sent by God--my new guardian and companion.

When we got back, my new buddy followed me into the main building and I started thinking about feeding him. He didn't look particularly hungry or undernourished, but he was a big dog and probably required a significant amount of daily fare. I knew that to feed dogs people food was not a healthy option for them and so I started to worry. I returned to the kitchen and started opening cupboards I had not looked into earlier. I was looking for rice as I seemed to remember that you could boil beef and rice to make dog food. But I was astonished to find in one of the lower cabinets a whole stock of dog food--kibble, cans of wet food, and biscuits. And it suddenly dawned on me that La Playa was Fella's home, that whomever it was who tended to this lost DHS resort had a pet on this lonely island to keep him company. As if in confirmation of this, when I went back into the lounge area, I found Fella curled up comfortably on one of the couches with a rawhide bone that he had retrieved from its hiding place between his paws. He definitely looked at home.

So, there went my hopes of finding some friendly family to whom Fella belonged, nice people who would call the FBI or someone to get me out of here. Plan B seemed to be a return to plan A: Wait. Fella and I would hang in here, together, in the rather tenuous hope that someone, somewhere, knew we were here and would eventually do something, anything, to get us the hell out of here.

Meanwhile, I had to revise my thinking and decided that for whatever reason, Timmy and company had considered this a safe place for me--if not for them--and that, thus far, even after the disappearance of my minder (or minders), I still did seem to be relatively "safe." Alone, but alone with dog, supplies, and no apparent intruders, stalkers, kidnappers, or visible enemies. A telephone would have been nice.

I pondered whether I should move from the cottage into the main building, whether I should perhaps occupy one of the empty bedrooms on the second floor and sort of combine the living spaces of Fella and myself into this one space. I called to Fella to follow me to my cottage wishing to see how he'd respond. He jumped off the couch with his bone still in his mouth and followed me along to the cottage and, when I went inside, he followed me in and almost immediately jumped up on the couch and resumed chewing. So, I thought, I'll just stay put, stay where they had initially wanted me, and Fella and I would sleep in the cottage, commute to the inn for meals and lounge time, maybe even hang out on the beach and play fetch. I thought I would feel safe with Fella there with me. A gal and her dog.

And for three more days, this is exactly what we did.

21

When Fella got me up on the fourth day of my exile, he seemed rather unusually excited or alert. Rather than just gently pawing my face, which was his usual wake-up call, on this morning he jumped up onto the bed and did a little dance, turning little circles this way and that. Just seconds later, there was a knock at the cottage door. My heart kind of stopped. Half awake, I tried to think, plan, guess, anticipate. But the knock came again, louder this time, and Fella started yelping. So I staggered out of bed, pulled the jacket of my now well-worn track suit on over my nightgown, and made my way to the door, saying, inanely, yes, yes, coming. Who did I think I was talking to? And then I opened the door, and standing there on the doorstep was Timmy and, merciful God, Emily too.

I think I kind of cried or screamed or, like Fella, yelped.

Emily grabbed both my arms, maybe I looked faint, I probably did, and led me to the couch, and sat me down. She retrieved some orange juice from the fridge and made me drink. Timmy, looking rather tired and sheepish, still dressed in his khakis and black sweater, flopped into one of the armchairs and let me drink. Fella just ran around, back and forth from one of us to the other, clearly ecstatic with all the action.

So, Timmy said, when I finished drinking my juice: You survived. I refrained from any wise remarks like, yes, and no thanks to you, and said nothing. So, Timmy continued, the explanation is long and, at the moment. . . I know, I interrupted. Confidential, need to know, etcetera. He smiled at me and said: something like that and then said that we'd be leaving as soon as I wanted to and could get ready. How about five minutes, I said? But then I looked at him again and said, what about Fella? Who, said Timmy? The dog, I said. The dog who kept me sane for four days. Oh, he's coming with us, he said. The guy who takes care of this place is a retired agent, lives on a nearby island, helps us out when we need it. This is his dog. We left him to take care of you, but never any real danger, you know.

Timmy and Emily left me alone to get ready to go, but Fella stayed behind. I had a quick shower and shampoo while Fella worked his bone on the couch. I towel dried my hair, and then improvised my clothing. I wore slacks from the black pants suit and a roomy tee shirt I had found in a display cabinet at the inn. It was white, long-sleeved, with a map of Florida outlined on the front and then three large house keys superimposed on the map. I had thought it clever but chose to wear it now because it was new and clean, more than could be said for the rest of my tired wardrobe. I brushed out my damp hair, put on my sneakers, and then, hopefully, for the last time, packed my case. Emily came back to claim me and I felt moved to ask her how she was feeling. She said she was on sick leave and would be for another month, healing slowly, but healing, no permanent damage. She said, however, that she had begged to come along on this mission so she could see me safely home. I squeezed her arm and said how happy her cat would be to have her for a month and Emily, woman of few words, just smiled back and maybe had a tear in her eye. She looked thinner and had the remains of what had been a nasty bruise on her face, but she seemed otherwise functional--and I knew to question her no further.

Timmy came in after that to fetch my case, but instead of heading out to a golf cart or a walk to the air strip, we walked across the beach and down to the dock where a very spiffy cruiser was now idling, ready to set out to sea. Fella was the first to run up the gangway and then charge into the wheelhouse where he was reunited with a man who was presumably his owner. Fella was doing his full-out paws on shoulders act and nuzzling his snout into the man's neck and the man was saying, hey Duke, good fellow. So, he was "Duke." But he was indeed a very good fellow, too, I thought.

The man was introduced to me simply as Bert, a pleasant looking man in his 60s, probably, tall, spare, the look of the sea in his eyes. I thanked him for Fella--Duke--and he said he thought Duke had enjoyed "the mission." Well, he's a very good dog, I said, and found myself thinking that I would dearly miss his company.

Our sea voyage was relatively brief but pleasant, calm in the balmy weather and cool sea breezes and within a few hours, I found myself back on land and, eventually, at the Miami International Airport, about to board a commercial air flight, first class, bound for Newark. It had been exactly one week since my arrest but of course seemed like a lifetime.

As I settled into my very comfortable first-class seat next to Emily and Timmy and buckled myself in, I shook my head slightly, kind of trying to grab hold of this new, normal reality--or, to be more accurate, of this old reality, actually, which had been my nice, quiet, nothing life before the body in the shed changed it all. But not forever, I thought. Not forever.

We took off, ate, landed, got into yet another black SUV--and headed home.

AFTERWARD

My homecoming was somewhat anticlimactic given the events of the past week. On the positive side, Jared and Terrance were waiting for me there at my house and it was lovely hugging them both, long and strong. My double and all traces of her seem to have been removed and everything was orderly and shiny clean. And, after a bit of persuasion, I was also able to lure out the cats who had been in their usual shelter zone under my bed. Terrance informed me that they had spent much of the last week in there, but had deigned, eventually, to come out for meals. I just sat with both of them on my lap and buried my face in their warm fur, listening to them try to out-purr each other.

But in some small way, my house seemed a little foreign to me, like a place vaguely remembered but still strange. I couldn't shake the feeling that this had been a place of danger and implicit violence, a shelter and then a fortress that had been breached, and I wondered when I would be able to think of it as my "safe house" once again.

Timmy told me that "the DHS investigation" had finally been fully successful, had ended with a series of many arrests that would certainly lead to prosecutions and long prison sentences. He said that after I got settled and rested, we would have a de-briefing and that I would be told as much as he was able to tell me without breaching security and this news went a long way to dispel any immediate feelings of danger or threat.

I retired to my bedroom leaving Timmy in the breakfast room to talk with Jared and Terrance. Proverbially, I just wanted to be alone. I had nothing to unpack as I had left the suitcase with all my padded clothes and elevated shoes in Emily's custody. We had dropped her off at a place near her home where another SUV waited to take her the rest of the way and God knows what she did with my case. Burned it, I hoped. I took a long hot shower, luxuriating in the aroma therapy of my Jo Malone shower gel, shampooing my silly short brown hair again, and then wrapping myself in my big, soft bath towel and sinking on to my bed, my *own* bed, I thought. We had all arranged to go out for dinner that evening to celebrate my homecoming, as Jared put it. Meanwhile, I let myself drift off into one of those half-asleep, half-awake zones, restful, relaxing, until I began to feel at home, really at home for the first time in months. My relief came in waves, comforted me, calmed me.

We had a pleasant dinner, just Jared and Terrance and me. Timmy had begged off, saying he'd return in a few days to chat. So we three went to a lovely restaurant in an old restored Victorian mansion called La Grange, enjoyed cocktails, some shared appetizers, steaks and fries for the men and lamb chops and asparagus for me. I told them a bit about my week's adventure, but left out some things that I thought might border on the "confidential" (God, I was beginning to sound like Timmy). They loved the part about Duke, aka Fella, and I said I really missed that sweet companion still. We dropped Jared at the bus which would take him to the airport to catch a red-eye flight home. He just kept saying to me, it's all over mom, it really is--as much to convince himself as to comfort me, I think. I just hugged him tighter and said, I know, I know. And then I told him to thank Lucy for sharing him with me for all this time.

I slept like the dead that night and awoke in the morning to two kitties gently pawing my face, two starving kitties, as usual. I guess I'm really home, I thought, and smiled.

Timmy kept his promise and returned in a few days after first calling to secure a meeting time. I had been planning to go visit Martha, but wanted to meet with Timmy first--to query my status and get my marching orders.

We sat in the breakfast room over coffee and sugared blueberry muffins and Timmy told his tale--or some of it--and what a tale it was. He said the criminals under their pursuit were human traffickers. I was surprised, had always thought it would be a drug cartel. But these were a very special and deadly type of human traffickers, Timmy explained. It was a new enterprise, a kind of "boutique business" that actually took "orders" for the desired human or humans and then kidnapped or snatched people, mostly children, to fill those "orders." The clients were international and the operation was insidious and very well organized. Victims were transported, sometimes hundreds or even thousands of miles to holding houses where they were imprisoned and "groomed" to the requirements of the new owners. Most of these owners had perverted and evil intent, most often sexual, but some were actually people who just wanted to adopt a child but had been unsuccessful. So children were stolen and provided to them. But in every case, these designer victims yielded fortunes, sometimes as much as a million dollars for, say, a young, blond boy, preferably about five or six years old. My heart ached as Timmy talked. I had known, as we all know, about the horrors of human trafficking, but somehow, Timmy's narrative put the "human" part of it in a new perspective and made me sick as well as incredibly sad.

Apparently my new neighbors, Tad and Mariah Worthington, were building and about to operate one of the holding houses for which they would receive ten percent of the profit from every soul they housed. Built into the hillside under that lovely modern home they were constructing were, veritably, four holding cells, underground and soundproof, where sweet Tad and svelte Mariah would "groom" (terrorize, brainwash) the merchandise. Willie Arthur, the body in my shed, had been a sort of low-level go-fer for the Worthingtons but when he sort of sniffed out what they were doing, he tried to blackmail them which ended with his being shot, most likely by Tad, and placed in my shed, away from the workers. Timmy thought they had intended to move the body again, but that I discovered him before they could. Careless, said Timmy, very careless, but then Tad and Mariah were relative amateurs in the criminal world. They took a pot shot at your friend Martha, too, just to try to confuse the Arthur death, make it looks like some serial shooter in the neighborhood. Thank God they weren't very good shots.

As for further information about where I had been for the past week or what had caused the disruptions in out travels, Timmy was vague, so I let it go. He seemed especially unwilling to talk about his hasty departure and disappearance from the island in the Keys, some sort of emergency part of the operation that required him and Bert to speed off and leave me Duke. In the clandestine world of his operations, I assumed all did not always go smoothly. It was what it was and I had, after all, been kept safe--from Tad and Mariah and any others in the enterprise who wished me ill--if rather jostled in the process. As for what I was supposed to say about all this, he said that about my arrest I was just to say that it had been a legal and clerical error, totally without merit, and that such a report had been printed unobtrusively in local newspapers, in case anyone was looking. As for the trafficking ring--and Mariah and Tad's involvement--I was to say absolutely nothing to anyone, even Terrance and Jared. They both knew some basic facts, just enough to understand the need for my absence. Timmy felt that the story would break in the papers soon--and that I should read those news stories and discuss only what was written there, if the subject ever came up with anyone, and talk about nothing of what he had told me. As far as the wide world was concerned, I had been mistakenly sequestered in my home for the week following my bail hearing. I really understood it all, and I agreed. He assured me that my name would never be connected with the operation, ever.

And the bullet in my suitcase, I asked, almost jokingly? I put it there, Timmy said, a little B and E into Jared's house the night before you left. We hadn't quite ruled you out at that point, thus the San Diego contact, and why I needed to sneak into Jared's house to plant some bait, see what you'd do. He assumed that the mystery phone calls had been from Tad, just to try to shake me up--as had the nocturnal visit to my garden. Ah, so, I said. And that's all I said. Finally finished with his revelations, Timmy finished his muffin and coffee, got up to go, and surprisingly, gave me a large hug and patted my head. He then gave me a lopsided smile and said he hoped we'd never have to meet again. And I said: No offense, Timmy, but I also fervently hope so too. Although, I liked him and would miss him, and said so.

So he went, life resumed, Martha got well.

Every so often, I sit on my deck and look up at the hill above me where construction on the new house has resumed. The property's ownership had been discreetly transferred and sold and apparently I was to get new neighbors after all. But truth to tell, I am in no hurry to meet them.

CPSIA information can be obtained
at www.ICGtesting.com
Printed in the USA
LVHW110957150421
684615LV00007B/110

9 781665 521642